IRISH LIFE AND CULTURE

XV

IRISH FOLK CUSTOM AND BELIEF

nósanna agus piseoga
na ngael

le

seán ó súilleabháin

Arna chur amach do Chomar Cultúra Éireann
fé chomairca na dTrí gCoinneal Teo.
ISBN : 978-1-78117-935-2
Transferred to Digital Print-on-Demand in 2024

IRISH FOLK CUSTOM
AND BELIEF

by

SEÁN Ó SÚILLEABHÁIN

PUBLISHED FOR THE CULTURAL RELATIONS COMMITTEE
OF IRELAND AT THE THREE CANDLES, LTD.

INTRODUCTORY NOTE

THE aim of this series of booklets is to give a broad, vivid and informed survey of Irish life and culture, past and present. Each writer is left free to deal with his subject in his own way and the views expressed in any booklet are not necessarily those of the Committee.

Seán Ó Súilleabháin has for many years been Archivist and Registrar of the Irish Folklore Commission and is an internationally accepted authority on Irish folk tradition.

CONTENTS

ILLUSTRATIONS

IRISH FOLK CUSTOM AND BELIEF

FOREWORD

(a) The Nature of Folklore

BEFORE ENTERING UPON the questions of Irish folk belief and custom, it may be well to say a few words about the nature of folklore itself, of which they form a part. Folklore is a very comprehensive term to connote the complex of oral traditions of all peoples. It embraces not only their popular beliefs and customs, but also their traditional tales, legends, songs, proverbs, prayers, charms and riddles—in fact, any type of oral literature which has a more or less set form. It also includes local social history or *seanchas*, as it is called, and it can contribute to a science such as ethnology by providing material for a study of the ways in which people have lived in the past.

Because of its antiquity and continuity, folklore can make a helpful contribution towards the study of human history. It forms a valuable connecting link with the far-distant past. It owes its origin to what has been termed the folk—the quiet, secluded section of all peoples—who have evolved it, and kept it alive, over a long period of time. Professor Reidar Christiansen of Oslo has likened the folk to a quiet mountain lake, which retains only some of what it receives and rejects what it does not absorb. They have always lived in a conservative fashion and look with distrust upon everything new.

Any novel ideas which may happen to be accepted seep into the folk mind only very gradually and are received with caution. The folk have always been inclined to keep to the old ways of living, and this conservatism, as well as the sustained continuity of their ways of thinking, gives additional value to the lore they have preserved. Folklore belongs essentially to that inner section of peoples everywhere whose activities and thoughts are concerned only with their own environment and their daily interests. When they do adopt new ideas, they fit them into the homely, traditional mould, reshaping them, if necessary, to suit the pattern. The amalgam of lore thus accumulated and retained is somewhat like the contents of an antique shop, crammed with objects of different ages, and lacking in any evident order or cohesion.

Folklore is one of the oldest and most international inheritances of the human race. It brings us into close touch with a mentality that embraces all countries and all times. It must not be regarded as the debris of any system of religion or theology, but as a continuation and survival of a very ancient way of thinking. Underlying its patchwork and seemingly disordered pattern is a deep, silent substratum of folk thought, which serves to maintain an unbroken link with primitive mentality, from which most religious systems as well as most spiritual culture have ultimately sprung.

Old though folklore be in its origins, it is nevertheless a living thing. It is continually changing and developing at a slow rate by incorporating new ideas—sometimes several centuries after they have been generally accepted by others. Such innovations are welcomed by the folk mind only if they are in a kind of harmony with what is already there. For example, the so-called " wise men " and " wise women ", who were both highly respected and feared by our grandfathers in rural districts, were directly descended, in so far as their craft was concerned, from the men and women who won fame in the Middle Ages as magicians, with the rise of black magic and witchcraft, and these later practitioners derived their potpourri of "wisdom" and medical knowledge from the well-thumbed manuals of the medieval schools. This type of lore seemed to suit the folk mind and was absorbed by it.

It may be said here, by way of parenthesis, that even in the field of oral literature, the folk reject what does not fit into the traditional mould. The ballads, for example, which spread all over Europe some hundreds of years ago, never gained more than a very slim and precarious footing in either Ireland or Finland, because both of those countries had their own strong schools of native poetry. Similarly, a folktale will be accepted and make its way into the general repertoire of storytellers in any country only if it is good of its kind and accords with the types of tales which are popular there.

Folklore is a link with the past in a deeper sense than are old records or archaeological remains. It leads us, Christiansen says, not to the bare skeleton of what was once alive but to the innermost mind of mankind. It has preserved many elements whose origins must be sought in remote antiquity. It is by no means a codification of traditional rules, beliefs and customs, but a conglomeration of all of these, each having its own separate explanation and background. Some have certainly been derived from pre-christian times; others have been changed through the medium of the Christian church; while still others—as folklore is a living thing—have come into being only in comparatively recent times. Though old

9

as a world phenomenon, folklore seems destined to continue to live according to its own rules as long as man shall inhabit this earth.

One final word about those who keep traditional lore—tales, songs, customs, beliefs and such things—alive. Even when our native culture was at its strongest, using the Irish language as its vehicle, the number of good storytellers or singers in any rural community was relatively small. True, there were far more than these who could, but rarely or never did, tell tales and sing songs. The tradition in both fields was kept alive and handed on by the few active bearers of it. It was so too with custom and belief—it was a small inner core of persons, within a sympathetic community, who kept these things intact and passed them on to succeeding generations. Folk medicine is a good example of this: the traditional knowledge and practice of it was, in any parish, in the hands of a comparatively small number of "wise" men and women, who added depth and breadth to the superficial knowledge of the bulk of the community.

The notion that all the folk in common were the bearers of all belief and custom/tradition is as wrong as to postulate that all of the folk in common invented their traditional tales or composed their songs and kept them alive before passing them on to those who came after them. No, it is to the active (not the passive) tradition-bearers among the ordinary people of Ireland and elsewhere that we owe thanks for the valuable stock of lore which has come down to us through the ages.

(b) Folk Custom and Belief in General

Folk belief and custom are, to my mind, the most interesting parts of folklore. The haphazard collecting of them has been going on in many countries for upwards of a century, but attempts to assess their content and to study them scientifically began only about sixty years ago.

Folk beliefs, as Christiansen has pointed out, were, in their origins, highly practical measures, deeply concerned with human life and welfare. Far from being casually evolved, they were in the main serious attempts to protect vital human interests and were relied upon by the folk in times of crisis or danger, whether fancied or real. Like religion, they answered a need in the lives of the people. In times of stress and doubt, such trusted traditional expedients brought comfort, if not relief. In early times, man felt insecure, as he lived—so he seemed to think—under the shadow of unknown powers, some of whom he regarded as hostile. Although life in general has now become more secure, still superstition will always be present to some degree, even among advanced societies.

Its conservatism is one of the chief characteristics of folk belief. Our ancestors thought it risky to depart from the old, tried precautions of former generations. This gave a kind of compactness and unity to their traditional beliefs, which seemed to be controlled and directed by some hidden under-tow or current, which continually turned their thoughts and feelings in a certain direction and prevented a too ready acceptance of new ideas.

It is race and mode of life which give folk belief its special colour. This is not so with oral literature, however, whose character is determined more by geographical position than by anything else. Again, people cling to old ideas far more tenaciously than they do to stories and songs. Indeed, only a major change in the pattern of life of a people, such as that caused by famine, plague, war, invasion, colonisation or mass migration, will radically affect the customs and beliefs of the rural population.

Folk belief, in the sense of superstition, was bound to be at variance with modern cultural outlooks, and has been opposed through public education, as well as through religious teaching and other means, not excluding ridicule. New states of society all over the world have looked upon such antiquated survivals as impractical and absurd, if not pagan, once they had become detached from their original, practical purpose. It must be stressed, however, that even today they have value as proofs and examples of an older condition of culture, out of which a newer one has been evolved. Some survivals lead us back to the habits of hundreds and even thousands of years ago; all are worthy of a sympathetic approach and study for the light they may throw on the mental processes of our ancestors.

In a sense, folk belief is a correlative of the science of higher cultures. It tries in its own way to find answers to many questions about life and the world in general. Although it does this wrongly, it has, however, a certain kind of logicality. It bases its judgements on emotion rather than on reason, using wrongly-grasped ideas of coincidence, association, similarity, contrast and connection. More of this later—for the present one example will suffice: it was believed that by injuring some garment or possession of an enemy, the owner would also suffer similar injury. Such reasoning, if we may term it so, must seem irrational to more educated minds. Still, although such aspects of folk belief led to many incon- sistencies, the system worked in a very unified way and provided the folk with a fairly harmonious outlook on life.

A closer examination of the lines of reasoning along which folk beliefs grew will quickly reveal that they display a praise- worthy degree of logic for the various times at which they came into being. The folk had not the opportunities which we have of making sufficiently close or numerous observations in order to discover what we today term the laws of nature. They were for that reason unable to make scientifically correct interpretations of various natural phenomena. The explanations which we deem evident, with the aid of natural science, were beyond their powers, owing to their poorer qualifications. Still, the folk regarded Nature, as we do, as something subject to laws. The difference between their explanations and ours is merely that the laws according to which they tried to explain what happened followed a kind of mysticism, a belief in the powers of magic to control those of Nature. There was a belief, for example, that like produces like: a woman who possessed certain special powers could, it was thought, by stirring water violently in a vessel, raise a storm at sea; a fisherman becalmed at sea could raise wind by whistling for it; or an ailment could be cured by reciting a charm telling how Jesus had cured a similar ailment.

The folk did not appear to have been aware of the chance of coincidence. If, for example, a fisherman on his way to the sea met a fox or a red-haired woman or a priest and failed to catch any fish that day, the fox or the woman or priest was blamed and their like were avoided by fishermen in the future. Similarly if somebody died shortly after seeing a ghost or after being frightened in some other way, it was believed that the ghost had come to take him off into the world of the dead, rather than that he had died from some natural cause. The folk always looked for a cause for every happening and often reached wrong conclusions.

When we come to examine folk customs a very rich variety is revealed. Some of them can readily be seen to be of a purely social character, kept alive by popular fashion. Examples of these for Ireland would include strawboys at weddings, and "Biddies" who go from house to house on the eve of the Feast of St. Brigid (Feb. 1). A second group of folk customs is associated with work on the farm: placing the spade in the fire at the conclusion of the potato digging, or taking home the last sheaf of the harvest in triumph. Many customs, however, are based on folk belief, as is clear from the fact that the beliefs in question have lived on into our own time. It often happens nevertheless that a custom may be kept up long after the folk belief which gave rise to it had disappeared (the playing of games at wakes, which will be mentioned later, is an example of this). People have continued some customs, at one time firmly established and understood, without asking themselves why they did so. This can sometimes cause a custom to be cut off from its origin, so that people can no longer discern its basic reason. They may then ask themselves why they do this or that, and the answer they give is a wrong one, thus giving rise, in its turn, to a change in the custom itself. It is always unsafe to detach a custom in this way from its hold on the past, treating it as an isolated fact to be simply disposed of by some plausible explanation. Thus a festival custom, the original reason for which has been forgotten and lost, may easily become transferred to other festivals with which it may have no basic connection, and which it may not even suit.

Since the still-living belief grew out of an ancient process of folk-reasoning, quite independent of modern knowledge, a large part of folk custom is in its origins incapable of explanation by the folk themselves. In order to understand such forgotten beliefs, it is necessary to carry out comparative research. A folk custom may vary from place to place in the way in which it is observed. It can change its place in the calendar, as has been mentioned, or be added on to something to which it does not properly belong. A new or a mistaken interpretation of a custom can change it also. Only a comparative study can sometimes show what is original and what is a later change or accretion.

In a booklet of this size, it is not possible to do more than take a superficial look over the field of Irish folk belief and custom. Some representative examples of both will be chosen, but thousands will of necessity have to be omitted. Not one volume, but a whole library, would be needed to cover these subjects in depth.

As popular pastimes such as storytelling, singing, dancing, the playing of games and other amusements do not properly belong to the field of folk custom as described in this booklet, I have decided not to include them.

I. HOUSE AND HOME

IT IS QUITE evident from the numerous stories which were told about houses which seemed to be unlucky for some unknown reason that people in olden times placed the main blame on the wrong choice of site. This might be due to the house having been built on a path which should have been left clear for the fairies to use in their passage from one *lios* ("fairy fort") to another, or else on the site of a *lios* itself. It followed naturally, according to the folk's way of thinking, that such a house would be haunted and unlucky. Neither should a house be built on the site of a former forge, nor on a height.

Many precautions were taken to avoid trouble when building a new house. The advice of a "wise" person (who was supposed to have special knowledge) was sought as to which site was right from the point of view of the super-natural beings who lived "outside of the people". Another plan was to mark the four corners of the proposed site with stones or sticks—if these were left in position overnight, the building could proceed. A new house to replace the old one should not be built at the other side of the road. Nor should a room be built, as an extension, "west" of the house.

Much has been written about the widespread custom, in Ireland and elsewhere, of burying something under the foundation stones of houses. There is evidence of animal heads, empty vessels, coins, holy medals and other objects having been placed under the foundation stones of castles and dwelling-houses. The custom has been variously explained by the wish to placate the disturbed spirit of the site, or else (in the case of human or animal sacrifice) to provide a

FARMSTEAD IN COUNTY GALWAY

THE CORN HARVEST

guardian spirit for the house. Archaeological excavations show that the custom is many thousands of years old in some countries. It must be stated, however, that the burial of empty vessels and horse-skulls under floors and in walls has also been explained as an endeavour to provide the building with a resonant sound for dancing, threshing and other activities.

It is commonly said in Ireland that bull's blood was used in the mixing of mortar for the building of castles. Whether this was so or not, it is certain that a white stone or any stone which fell from a builder while working would not be inserted in a house-wall. Nor should the stones of an old house be used as material for the walls of a new one (this may partly explain why so many ruined houses are left standing after being deserted).

When taking possession of a new house, the time was carefully chosen. The move would not take place in Lent on any account. Friday now seems to be the lucky day for taking possession, but an old saying restricts even this: a move to the north on Friday, to the south on Monday, or to the west on Tuesday never brought any luck in its train. Some coals of fire from the old house were often taken into the new one, but the *croch* (chimney-crane for hanging cooking vessels on) was always left behind. So too was the cat, unless it was sent to the new home a few days previously.

In olden times, the fire was both physically and socially at the centre of the house. As turf-fires, which were the norm in most parts of rural Ireland, were smoored (covered with ashes) each night and so kept alive until next morning, there is good reason to yield to the claim that many domestic fires remained burning for hundreds of years. A prayer such as the following was commonly recited when the live embers were being covered with ashes at night:

Coiglim an tine seo mar choigleann Críost cáidh ;
Muire ar mhullach an tí, agus Bríd ina lár ;
An t-ochtar aingeal is tréine i gCathair na nGrás
Ag cumhdach an tí seo 's a mhuintir thabhairt slán.

(I save this fire, as noble Christ saves ; Mary on the top of
the house and Brigid in its centre ; the eight strongest angels
in Heaven preserving this house and keeping its people safe.)

As the prosperity of the house and farm was thought to be
closely associated with the fire, every effort was made, especially
on May Day (the start of Summer), to keep the fire intact
from evil-minded persons. So too, the fire was symbolic of
human life ; if anybody was ill in the house, the fire was not
allowed to die down during that time.

Various objects were also hung up in houses or kept there
to ensure good luck and protection. A caul, clay from Tory
Island off the coast of Donegal, or house-leek would save the
house from being burned ; the elder tree, which grew near
many houses, would protect them, it was thought, from
lightning ; the skin of a king-otter would avert general harm ;
the shoe of an ass, St. Brigid's crosses, blessed palm, holy
(Easter) water, or a black cock (which had its perch over
the door inside) would ward off sorcery and harm by
supernatural beings ; a black cat, crickets or freak eggs
(placed inside the roof) would ensure luck for the house ;
and bunches of yarrow collected on the eve of the Feast of
St. John (June 24), as well as May flowers (but not
whitethorn), would keep illness and misfortune away.
As well as these positive precautions to preserve luck in the
house, people were also careful not to sweep out the floor-dust
on a Monday, lest they sweep out their luck also.

18

II. FARMER, FISHER AND CRAFTSMAN

IN OLDEN DAYS in Ireland, hunting must have contributed substantially to the support of the people. It is now such a long time since the population became settled, rather than nomadic, however, that relatively little custom and belief concerning hunting has survived.

The land has for a long time been the main source of Irish food supplies. In early times, grain crops came to be extensively cultivated, to be followed by the potato a few hundred years ago. The fertility of the land, as well as the preservation of that fertility, were all important in the eyes of our ancient ancestors. It is not to be wondered at, therefore, that a large body of folk custom and belief came to be associated with these two aspects of agriculture.

It was a general belief that the presence of a "fairy fort" or of a "fairy well" on a farm meant that the land would be fertile. To preserve this necessary quality, certain steps had to be taken: salt was sprinkled on a field before a crop was sown in it; so too was water in which a plough "sock" or coulter had been immersed (perhaps due to the belief that iron had special magical qualities). The christianisation of such customs as these can be seen in the later sprinkling on the land of holy water (blessed on Rogation Days, on Ascension Thursday or on Whit Sunday). When bonfires were lighted on May Eve or on St. John's Eve (June 23), the farm would either be encircled with fire by taking burning reed-sheaves around it to ward off evil influences, or else some burning bushes or sticks from the fires were thrown over the fence into the fields where crops were growing; similarly, in the

19

areas where the May-bush custom prevailed, branches from the bush were thrown among the crops. It was even believed that the fertility of a neighbour's holding could be stolen from him by secreting eggs or raw meat (or the dead body of some animal) on his land—as these decayed, so did his prosperity, by a process of sympathetic magic.

There is ample evidence from Ireland and Europe that dead bodies were not allowed to be taken for burial through the land of others; special laws were passed against this in several countries. The basic reason seems to have been the belief that the passage of a corpse brought ill-luck to land and crops.

There is not space in this booklet to enumerate the many customs and beliefs associated with the planting and care of crops. Let one suffice: it was deemed very unlucky to miss a line in a ridge when planting seed-potatoes—the whole crop and even the general prosperity of the farm might be threatened.

The securing of the harvest, no matter what the crops were, was a crucial period of the agricultural year. It will not surprise us, therefore, that when this operation was finally completed, great celebrations took place. The spade was ceremonially placed in the fire to signify that it was no longer needed, once the potato crop had been dug. Even at the end of a long period of spinning, part of the spinning-wheel was similarly put into the fire. They would, however, be quickly rescued from the flames by the woman of the house, who was then expected to prepare a feast for the workers. This celebration was known as the *féil searra* or *clabhsúr* (closure), and included drinking as well as feasting, singing, dancing and storytelling. It was purely a happy social occasion and not at all based on any folk belief. So too was the cutting of the last sheaf of the grain-crop, which was known by such various names as the "churn", the "granny", *an chailleach* (the old woman) and *an luchtar* (the bunch or sheaf). Sometimes the last sheaf was sent, mischievously, to some neighbour who was slower at reaping his crop; in most cases, however, it was taken home in triumph and placed on the beams of the kitchen during the feast, and harvest knots were woven from it later and worn by boys and girls.

Farm animals and their products helped also to balance the economy of rural communities in Ireland. These consisted mainly of cows and their produce, horses, donkeys, sheep, goats, pigs, as well as poultry and bees. The many customs and beliefs connected with all of these cannot be dealt with in a booklet of the present size. I have, therefore, decided to confine my remarks to the main type of farm animal, the cow, and her produce of milk and butter.

Almost all of the customs and beliefs in this field were concerned with the physical welfare of the cows and the warding off of diseases and other evils which might affect them harmfully. The cow-house or byre was built on a site which would not prevent the passage of fairies or encroach on their territory (mainly, the "fairy fort"). Crosses made of straw and other materials on St. Brigid's Eve were hung in the cowhouse or fixed to the doors and windows. It was hoped to protect the cows themselves by tying red ribbons to their tails or around their necks; rings made of rowan were similarly applied for the same purpose. Cattle were driven across the dying flames of bonfires on May Eve and St. John's Eve, or between two of these fires. So too they were forced to swim in a lake or river at certain times to avert illness and bad luck.

A goat was generally kept with herds of cows " to bring them luck ". I have heard this custom explained by saying that goats had the capacity for eating poisonous herbs without being fatally affected, which was not the case with cattle. Another animal which was regarded as lucky in a herd was a *maighdean bhuaile* (a cow which had never borne a calf). Holy water was, of course, often sprinkled on livestock, and scores of charms (apocryphal folk-prayers) were recited to avert or cure the many diseases from which they might suffer, whether through natural causes or, as the folk often suspected, through the evil eye of an unfriendly neighbour. The fairies too were blamed for causing animals to be " elf-shot ". This was due to the fact that ailing cows, with pierced hides, might be found grazing near a place where small stone arrow-heads from ancient times were often found lying about; the fairies were immediately blamed for having cast these weapons at the cows in an attempt to take them off into fairyland. One of the many remedies for " elf-shot " was to give the stricken animal a drink of water in which the " fairy arrows " had been boiled.

As soon as a cow had calved, she was ceremoniously blessed with holy water and fire, while the following prayer was recited three times :

Go mbeannaí Dia dhuit, a bhó !
Go mbeannaithear faoi dhó do do laogh !
Go mbeannaí an triúr atá i bhflaitheas Dé,
Mar atá : An t-Athair agus an Mac agus an Spiorad Naomh !
Tar, a Mhuire, agus suidh ; tar, a Bhríd, agus bligh ;
Tar, a Naomh Mícheál Ard-aingeal, agus beannaigh an mart

22

In ainm an Athar agus an Mhic agus an Spioraid Naofa,
Agus Amen, a Dhia.

(God's blessing on thee, O cow ! twice blest be thee, O calf !
May the Three who are in Heaven bless you : the Father and
the Son and the Holy Spirit ! Come, Mary, and sit down;
come, Brigid, and start milking; come, Blessed Michael,
the Archangel, and bless the beef. In the name of the Father
and of the Son and of the Holy Spirit. Amen, O God.)

Although it was commonly accepted that the fairies who
lived in the forts might need milk and take it from cows on
the farm, this was not resented, as people wished to live in
amity with their otherworld neighbours. Precautionary
measures were directed more against evil-minded neighbours,
who were liable to endeavour to steal one's milk- or butter-
" profit " *(sochar an bhainne)* by magic means. Newly-calved
cows stood in need of special protection, as their supply of
milk was assured. Crushed flowers, such as marsh marigold,
were rubbed to their udders, which were also singed with the
flame of a blessed candle. The first stream of milk drawn
from such a cow was allowed to fall on the ground " for those
who might need it " (the fairies, presumably), and then a
cross was marked on the cow's flank with some of her milk.

A charred sod of turf from the Midsummer bonfire was
placed in the milk-house as protection. The greatest care was
taken not to lose one's milk-luck through negligence, as
witness the following traditional tabus : don't give away any
milk on New Year's Day, on May Day, on any Monday or
on a Friday; don't lend a milk-vessel; don't take to fetch
water from the well a vessel which is milk-stained; when
such a vessel has been washed, do not throw the cleansing
water into a river or stream; don't give milk to a neighbour

unless salt has been put into it; don't allow milk out of the house, if anybody is ill there.

It was a traditional custom never to drink milk on Good Friday; even the baby in the cradle, it is said, had to cry three times on that day before milk was fed to it. Another old-time custom, when goats were very numerous, was to drink their milk in the belief that it cured tuberculosis. Ballykinlar in Co. Down and Goatstown in Co. Dublin were famous over a century ago in this regard, and thousands of patients came there, even from Scotland, to drink goats' milk.

Farmers were constantly afraid in days gone by that their milk and butter "profit" could be stolen from them by evil-minded hags, who either bailed a neighbour's well or dragged a cloth over the dew of his fields on May Morn, saying "Come all to me!" People sat up all night on May Eve to guard their wells and fields against such spells. It was believed in Ireland, as well as in many other countries, that such human hags had the power of changing themselves into hares and sucking the milk from the udders of cows. These hares could be shot, so it was thought, only with a "silver bullet" (a pellet made from a florin which had a cross-device on one face).

Just as at calving-time, precautions had to be taken at churning-time against the evil intentions and wiles of others. In the old days, there were no creameries in rural areas, and farmers churned their milk at home. The churn was deemed to be especially vulnerable to those who were thought to be disposed to steal the butter "profit". Every effort was, therefore, made to guard it against such enemies: a live cinder was placed under the churn (many churns had charred bottoms in olden times), as well as an ass- or horse-shoe; in other districts, nails of iron would be driven into the timber of the churn to protect it, or else a withy of rowan-tree was bound around it. The tongs were kept in the fire during the period of churning, and water or fire-ashes were not allowed out of the house until the operation had ended. So too, the fire was guarded: if anybody came to a house while churning was in progress and tried (by " reddening " his pipe or other- wise) to take live fire out of the house, he was prevented from doing so, and forced to take a " brash " (hand) at the churning before leaving—thus the churn and its butter were kept intact from harm. There were many other precautions which were normally taken on this important domestic occasion, but space does not allow of their mention here.

Along the sea-coast and in the vicinity of lakes and rivers, fishing served to partially replace or supplement the food won from the land. As water was a quite different element from the land, embarking on it and catching fish in it were hedged around with tabus, as well as other beliefs and customs. There is room here to mention but a few.

If fishermen on their way to the water met a woman (still worse if she happened to be red-haired or barefoot), they knew instinctively that they would catch nothing that day, and generally returned home. It was similarly regarded as unlucky to meet a hare, a rabbit, a priest, or a fox. Indeed, one way of ensuring that a fisherman would have no luck was to say to him:

> Sionnach ar do dhubhán,
> Girrfhia ar do bhaoite,
> 'S nár mharbha' tu aon bhreac
> Go Lá Fhéile Bríde.

(May there be a fox on your fishing-hook and a hare on your bait, and may you kill no fish until St. Brigid's Day !).

Much discussion of the probable bases for these ill-omens has been published by European scholars.

Fishermen had many tabus to cope with also. While fishing at sea, they were not supposed to mention a priest, a pig or a weasel (they had to be spoken of as " the man with the white collar", " cold irons" and " the noble little old woman", respectively). So too, when setting out for the fishing-grounds, they should not bail water out of the boat; three men of the same name should not fish together; and no fisherman should smoke while at work. And at home in his own house, he had to take care that a fish-bone was never thrown into the fire. Ill-luck was expected to ensue if these or many other tabus were broken.

Many beliefs and customs of a prechristian character were also associated with endeavours to ensure good luck while fishing. A branch of rowan or furze was often taken out in the boat, or sprigs of them were attached to the men's clothes. A green branch was also tied to the mast on May Morn for luck. A live coal from the fire was thrown after a fisherman as he left the house to give him good luck. Eating the first egg laid by a hen was another supposedly beneficial action, as was the strewing of shell-fish in the four corners of the house on St. Brigid's Day (a symbolic act to ensure a supply of fish each day during the fishing season). It was also believed that dipping a fishing-bait into water in which the flesh of a *corr-iasc* (crane-bird, noted for its ability to catch fish) had been boiled, or spitting on the bait would confer power on it.

Christianity gave rise to some very beautiful fishing customs : nets were lowered into the water in the name of God, Mary and St. Peter; the Rosary was generally recited in boats at sea at midnight, while the men waited to shoot or haul their nets; and as fishing boats passed wells and other places on shore which were deemed holy, the sails were lowered in salute.

Certain lakes and rivers were thought to be poor for fishing, ever since some saint or other had cursed them after being badly treated by fishermen there. Finally, there was a traditional tabu against fishing at sea on Saturday nights (this was probably due to the Church law regarding observance of the Sabbath). The Eve of the Feast of St. Martin (November 11) was a closed night, so far as fishing was concerned. John Boyle O'Reilly's well-known ballad about the drowning of many fishermen who ignored the tabu on the coast of Wexford is based on an historical occurrence. " The sea belongs to Martin on that night."

In former times, far more so than now, people depended on local craftsmen to supply them with goods and articles which they needed from time to time. There were thousands of blacksmiths, tinsmiths, carpenters, boat-builders, shoemakers, nail-makers, tailors (who went from house to house to work), manty-makers, thatchers, weavers, masons, millers, basket-makers and other tradesmen, who were normal and familiar figures in rural communities. Each of these crafts had its own particular body of traditional custom and belief associated with it.

For want of space, I shall have to confine myself to the blacksmith as an example of a rural craftsman. Possibly because of the comparatively new metal (iron) which was his medium, he was looked upon as a man of extraordinary powers—this attribution to him may well have been derived from the time when iron was first introduced to this country, over 2000 years ago. It was the proud boast of the smith that he was the only tradesman who could make his own tools. In rural areas, at least, special tribute was paid to him in the form of the head of each beef or other animal killed for food *(cuid an ghabha an ceann)*, as well as gifts of oats and straw. The smith was supposed to have power to cure diseases in man and animals—even forge-water was effective towards this end. He could banish evil spirits too. Above all, his curse was feared; woe betide anyone against whom the smith " turned the anvil ".

It is sad to think that such a useful and colourful member of the community has almost completely disappeared from the rural scene. Neither the articles which he forged for so long, nor his special powers in other fields, are needed in our modern age.

III. TRAVEL, TRADE AND COMMUNICATION

WHETHER TRAVELLING ON land or by sea, people always set out on their journey in olden times with a certain amount of anxiety. There were fears of danger of many kinds, not always originating from such human activities as highway robbery, which were common in the fairly recent past.

An Mhairbhne Phádhraic, an apocryphal folk-prayer, was recited as the journey began, and much faith was placed in its efficacy. Later came the sprinkling of holy water on the traveller as he left home, with a prayer like the following on his lips:

> *In ainm an Athar le bua*
> *Agus an Mhic a d'fhulaing an phian,*
> *Muire agus a Mac*
> *Go raibh liom ar mo thriall.*

(In the name of the victorious Father and of the Son Who suffered pain, may Mary and her Son be with me on my journey !)

As may be expected, travel was hedged around with numerous tabus and customs. Turn back if you meet a red-haired woman ; do not return for something you may have forgotten ; do not omit to take salt or a fire-ember or soot or a sprig of hazel or sally on your person to protect you against evil spirits ; if you meet a funeral, take three steps of mercy (*trí choiscéim na trócaire*) backwards with it. It was regarded as an omen of luck to find a white button on the road or to meet a hare or weasel. *Luan soir agus Máirt siar* (travel towards the east on Monday, towards the west on

Tuesday) was a well-known injunction. Small heaps (*cáirne*, cairns) of stones were occasional features of Irish roadsides and pathways until recent times; they marked places where somebody had died. Subsequent wayfarers were accustomed to throw a small stone on to the spot, with some prayer like the following one from Kerry:

Mo chloch sa leacht agus mo leas im' dhearnain.
Beannacht Dé le hanam m'athar agus mo mháthar,
Agus go háirithe le hanam an té cailleadh san áit seo!

(I throw this stone from my hand on the heap for good luck. May God bless the souls of my father and mother, and especially the soul of the person who died here!)

Crossroads played a prominent part in folk custom and belief, as well as in folktales. They were often burial places for unbaptised children and animals. At funerals, coffins were laid down at such places, and in Co. Wexford wooden crosses were placed on bushes by the roadside where roads met. Crowing hens, regarded as unlucky, were abandoned at crossroads too. Warts could be got rid of by leaving there stones which the sufferer had rubbed to them—the finder of the stones took over the warts. There are stories about people who gave themselves up to the Devil at crossroads. A more pleasant feature of Irish country life was the general custom, down to recent decades, of holding dances at such centres on Sunday evenings.

Travel over the sea was very hazardous in olden times when ships were smaller and less well-equipped than they are now. I knew an old Kerryman who, before dying at the age of a hundred, told me in Irish (he knew no English) that he had spent six months on board a sailing-ship trying to get to America; the ship had been blown three times across the Atlantic and three times back, without ever touching the American shore, so he never landed there at all! As well as taking food and utensils with them for the journey, emigrants also took hazel rods, and were careful never to set out on a Monday. "American wakes" were held before they left home, and the neighbours accompanied them on the first stage of their journey at the dawn of day. *An Mhairbhne Phádhraic*, already referred to, was recited to invoke good luck, and the travellers placed themselves under the protection of God and Colmcille.

Fishermen too, who used the sea, had their own customs and tabus. In the Shannon estuary, they made a pilgrimage around Scattery Island and carried some stone from that sacred place in their boats for luck. Waterford fishermen carried special loaves, known as St. Nicholas' Bread, with them for luck; an otter-skin and a caul were also carried in boats for added safety. A carpenter who made coffins was never asked to make a boat—the reason is fairly obvious—nor was a dead body, when found at sea, ever taken into a boat.

Country people had their own traditional methods of carrying on business. They counted fish, eggs, sheep, cabbage plants and many other things in special ways. So too, they measured cloth with finger-joints and fields in spade-lengths rather than yards. In Donegal, old people taking cattle to the fair, reckoned the length of the journey by the number of Rosaries they had recited as they went along.

Money was never as plentiful as people would have wished; what they had was hard-earned too. It was believed that certain coins (such as the florin with a cross on one face) and purses made from the skins of particular animals were lucky to possess. There were stories about coins which, no matter how often their possessor gave them away, always returned immediately to him. Coins were often spat upon for luck in buying and selling. When a horse was being purchased, the first part of the money paid for the animal was what had been received as the sale price of eggs or poultry—this was thought to bring luck to the animal. As may be expected, people were loth to part with any money on New Year's Day.

There is not space here to deal with the many traditional customs and beliefs which were associated with the making of bargains at fairs, when animals were being bought and sold. There were the hand-stroke, the luck-penny, the "earnest" money, the marking of the animals when bought, and several other traditional actions. When taking animals to a fair for sale, a shoe was thrown after the man of the house for luck, and he would even carry on his person some steel article which he had borrowed for the occasion. He would regard it as a bad omen to meet a hare or a red-haired woman on his journey. He also tied a red string or ribbon to the animals' tails, or knotted them for luck. When a farmer sold a horse, he always endeavoured to retain the halter. It was considered wrong to buy or sell an animal when going to a funeral or returning from one. A cart-load of turf always had a bush or emblem on top to denote that it was for sale.

As regards prices in general, people were wont to watch nearby rivers and streams on New Year's Day; a rising flood was an omen of rising prices, a falling one signified the opposite.

It was generally believed that the fairies mingled with people at fairs. They were visible, however, only to somebody who happened to have special sight through having "fairy ointment" rubbed to his or her eyes. When such a person

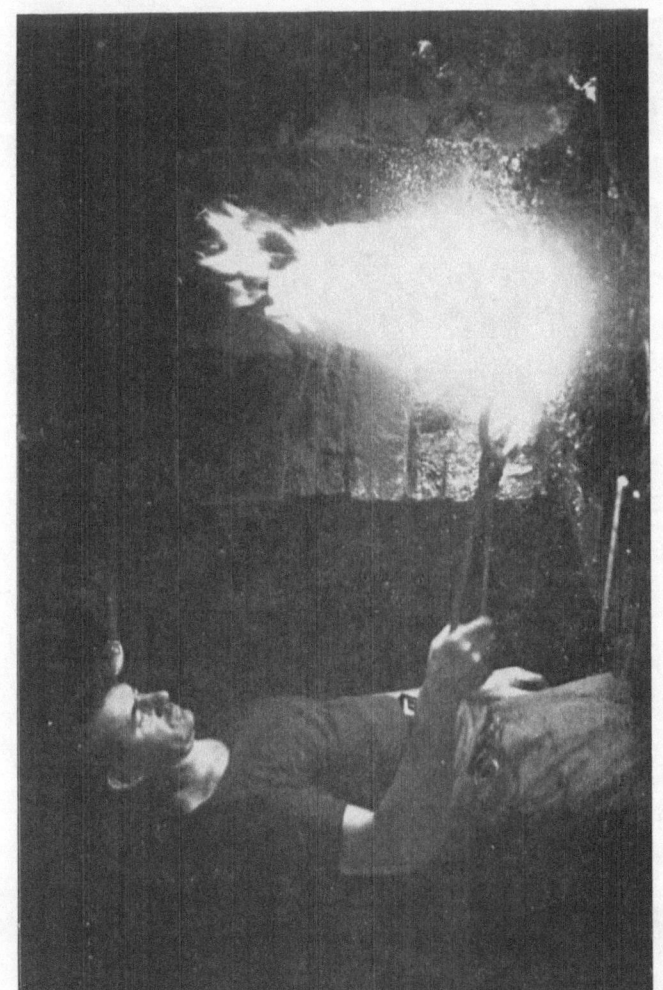

THE BLACKSMITH

BARGAINING AT A HORSE FAIR

spoke to a fairy man, thinking that he was human, the fairy man would discover, by questioning, which eye had the power of seeing him, and would quickly pluck it out! The fairies were often said, however, to have given poor farmers, under threat of eviction for non-payment of rent, money to pay the landlord; but when the landlord later went to count the money, he would find only some withered leaves!

We are nowadays so accustomed to the spreading of news and the giving of information by modern means (radio, telephone, telegraph, television, newspapers and so on) that we forget how difficult it must have been for our fore-fathers to communicate without these means. Mention can only be made here of the use of the spoken word for this purpose; messengers; fire, smoke, light or other visual signals; aural devices such as horn- or trumpet-blowing; the passing of tokens (as witness the story of Daniel O'Connell's boast that he could rouse all of Ireland in one night by sending *sifíní*—straws—from house to house), and so on. There were many customs, too, associated with the distribution of mail in olden times, as well as with the introduction of newspapers (when people gathered into houses to hear the schoolmaster or somebody else read the latest news for them). Such individuals also played an important part in the rural community by writing letters for those who could not do so in former times.

IV. THE COMMUNITY

THERE WERE MANY customs and beliefs associated with social relations within the community as a whole, and within the individual families which comprised it. A few topical examples are given below.

One of the most pleasant customs in rural Ireland was that termed *combar na gcombarsan* (mutual help given by neigh-bours). This help was always forthcoming whenever needed. Individual farmers " gave a hand " to one another in times of urgent need, and the compliment was repaid as occasion arose. An extension of this kind of mutual help was the *meitheal*, where a number of neighbours joined together for a day or two in helping, free of charge, someone who had a special type of work to be done : turf-cutting, harvesting and so on. The work was thus done more quickly, and the only charge on the person who received the help was the provision of food and, perhaps, some entertainment, when the task was completed. This man would on later occasions join other *meithleacha* in return, and thus a great spirit of cooperation existed in country districts.

Many well-to-do farmers who had not sufficient help within their own families would have recourse also to the hiring of servant-boys and servant-girls, who were paid for their work and also got their food. The main period of such employment extended from St. Brigid's Day (February 1), when Spring-work started, until Hallowe'en (October 31). Some servants would be kept on for the whole year, if required, and in this way, many of them in the old days earned their passage-money to America.

Another system for the employment of farm helpers was the following. Small farmers from West Cork, Kerry and West Connaught, left home in Spring each year, with their spades and a bundle of belongings on their shoulders, and walked long distances to towns in the South, the Midlands and Leinster, where "hiring fairs" were held at regular intervals. These men who offered themselves to large farmers for hire were known as *spailpíní* ("spalpeens"); they stood together in a corner of the fair, or near churches after Mass on Sundays, and were inspected for stamina by their potential employers. When a bargain about wages and conditions of employment had been struck, the hired men, either singly or in larger groups, accompanied their employer to his farm. The term of employment usually ended when the potato crop had been harvested in October, and the men returned to their homes, not only with their hard-earned wages, but also with new stories, songs and accounts of their experiences. Men from Mayo and Donegal generally went to the Lagan Valley in Ulster for work of this kind, or else crossed the sea to Scotland and England, returning home when the harvest there had been secured.

One hundred and fifty years ago, when the population of Ireland was much greater than it is now, country life was, despite many handicaps, both satisfying and colourful. While the native culture remained strong, storytelling, singing, dancing at crossroads and in houses, and games of various kinds (mainly hurling) took the place of the stereotyped amusements of today. People asked less of life then than we do now, and were possibly happier for that. The habit of visiting one another's houses was very common, and some houses were more popular than others as social centres. The custom has now ceased to a certain extent, as the fairly ubiquitous radio or television set tends to keep people at home. Public-houses were, of course, popular meeting-places too, and it was a widespread Irish custom to visit one on St. Patrick's Day to drink *pota Phádhraic* (St. Patrick's pot) with old friends. Weddings, wakes, funerals, fairs, " patterns " and sports meetings brought people together at intervals also, even though the main means of travel were confined to either foot or horseback.

In olden times children were not given the christian names of either of their parents in baptism, lest such would hasten the death of the parent in question. Rather, male children were named after either of their grandfathers; similarly, female children after their grandmothers or godmothers. If naming went outside of the traditional family pattern, it was known as *cúl le cine* (turning away from the ancestral line), and was resorted to only when successive babies died. When the Irish language was being replaced by English, traditional Irish names, such as Doncha, Diarmaid and Siobhán, were equated with Denis, Jeremiah and Joan (Hannah) respectively, with which they had no basic connection.

As regards surnames, when women married in rural Ireland in former times, they continued to be referred to by their maiden names—the term " Mrs. " was a later innovation. For private reasons too, certain families changed their surnames; in Kerry, I know of Greens who became O'Sullivans, Cliffords who took on the name of O'Brien, and so on. The Connaught family of O Laoi (Lee: *cf.* perhaps, Irish *liaigh*, a surgeon or physician) became famous as medical men, through, it is said, the possession of a book of medical knowledge acquired by one of them from supernatural sources. So too, it was commonly believed that the Cahills, Keoghs (Goughs), Darcys and Walshes had power to cure certain maladies by virtue of their surnames or their blood. Again, certain branches of the O'Sheas, Conneelys and Flaherties (as well as the McCodrums in Scotland) were closely involved with seals, ever since one of them had snatched her *cochall* (hood) from a mermaid and later married her—some of them were even believed to have webbed feet !

The Mass was in Christian times the main religious service and much traditional custom was associated with it. The old people had special traditional prayers which they recited on Sunday morning to welcome the day, as well as prayers which they said as they approached the church, entered it and left. Here is a sample:

> *Go mbeannaithear duit, a theampoll Dé,*
> *An áit a gcomhnaíonn mo Shlánathóir, Iosa Críost !*
> *Muire agus an dá asbal déag*
> *Ag guí orm féin inniu.*

(Hail to thee, O church of God, in which lives my Saviour, Jesus Christ ! May Mary and the twelve apostles pray for me today !)

And when leaving the church:

> *Beannacht leat, a Mhuire !*
> *Beannacht leat, a Chríost !*
> *Go gcumhdaidh sibh m'anam*
> *Go dtige mé arís.*

(Farewell, O Mary, and farewell, O Christ ! May ye preserve my soul until I come again !)

37

Such simple, beautiful prayers as these were in use on hundreds of different occasions, not in Ireland only but also in the Gaelic-speaking parts of Scotland, as is shown by Carmichael in the volumes of *Carmina Gadelica*.

Finally, the "Stations" *(tithe faoistine)* were, and still are, a normal part of Irish religious life. Twice a year, in Spring (mainly in Lent) and in Autumn, the parish clergy visited one house in each townland on a certain day, and there heard the confessions of all who attended, celebrated Mass and distributed Holy Communion. Parish dues were then collected, and both clergy and laity were entertained to breakfast. Thus, if there were, say, twelve houses in a particular townland, Mass was celebrated in each house once every six years—a privilege which is not accorded generally in other Catholic countries, and may have arisen in Ireland during Penal times, when public celebration of Mass was prohibited, and many priests were "on the run".

It is not to be wondered at that in popular belief the priest had not only powers conferred by the church, but was also believed to be able to perform many acts outside the scope of laymen. He could cure many ailments, overcome tyrants (such as landlords) by his magical powers, banish the Devil and other evil spirits, escape miraculously from pursuers and so on. "Silenced priests" (who had been suspended by their superiors for some reason) were supposed to be particularly effective in these ways; even their garments or clay from their graves were regarded as efficacious for certain purposes. And, strange to state, a newly-ordained priest was believed to have greater powers in many ways than even the highest of his superiors.

V. HUMAN LIFE

THE IDEA OF the existence of some kind of soul in human beings is found among even the most primitive peoples. The soul (as distinct from the life-force) was regarded as some kind of concrete entity, capable of moving about independently of the body to which it belonged, and of assuming different shapes at will. In Ireland, for example, there are traces of the belief that the souls of emigrants who had died abroad returned to their native land in the form of seagulls or in a sea-mist.

Such ideas were, of their nature, prechristian. Dreams and hallucinations among early peoples seem to have given rise to the belief that the soul (or whatever it was) could move about of its own accord. In dreams, we appear to see people and to speak to them, and they converse with us—it does not matter that some of them are already dead. Nowadays, we awake, knowing that it was only a dream. But early man, relying on the evidence of his senses, believed that it all had really happened. Thus there arose the idea that part of oneself could leave the body in sleep, meet its counterparts and associate with them, returning later to the body.

A common story in Ireland and elsewhere tells how an old man, accompanied by a young boy, went out into a field one fine day; the old man lay down and was soon fast asleep; the boy then saw a butterfly emerge from the old man's mouth and fly off towards a ruin in the bottom of the field; after a while, the butterfly returned and re-entered the old man's mouth; he immediately woke up and told the boy that he had dreamt that he had gone into that same ruin and there found hidden treasure; they both went immediately to the ruin and found the treasure at the place indicated in the dream.

From the type of belief which underlies the foregoing story—that the soul (butterfly, in this case) can leave the body when it sleeps—it is but a natural step to the belief that the souls of the dead can also move about. This came to be tied up with the idea of ghosts and the human fear of them, as they could sometimes be malignant.

Other ideas concerned the human blood, the breath, and the body's shadow, which were also associated with the life or soul. Also, in folktales, we meet with the motif of the giant's soul (life) being outside of his body, hidden in an egg. So too, the human life-index might be bound up with such a thing as a tree, which was planted when the person was born; when the tree began to fail and die, so too would the person.

Folk belief was never very clear, naturally, about what appearance the soul had, in itself. It was, however, believed that it entered the body at birth through *loigín an bhaithis* (the skull-cleft) and left by the same exit at death. It was believed that souls were so small that two of them could converse while doing their purgatory at either side of a leaf; so also they could congregate in great numbers on the rafters of houses. It was also said that a dead person should not be keened over for two hours after death lest the sleeping dogs of the Devil be roused along the path which the departed soul had to follow.

All over the world there is a traditional objection to unauthorised intrusions on certain occasions. For example, men should not intrude where women are working, and vice versa. There are many stories told to explain how certain castles came to be left unfinished: the builders had refused to complete the building after they had seen a woman stop to observe them at work. Then there is the story left unfinished by Cúchulainn when he discovered that a woman had been smuggled into a forge to listen to him, against his orders.

Reference has already been made to the aversion men had to meeting a red-haired woman, or one who wore a red garment, while on their way to fish or to a fair. A whistling woman or a crowing hen equally brought bad luck. An echo of the biblical story of Samson is to be found in the rule that a woman should not cut a boy's hair nor should she draw water from certain holy wells. It was said that if the gift of poetry descended to a woman it would end with her—she could not hand it on to her sons. In the field of folk medicine, some remedies had to be applied by a man to a woman, others by a woman to a man. Finally, when they came to die, men were said to meet Death quietly, while women resisted it *(deire fir a shuan, deire mná á faire féin suas)*.

Conception and childbirth have always been regarded as crucial points in human life, and so were hedged about with a great many beliefs and customs. It was said that sterility could be overcome by sleeping in the old remains popularly known as " beds of Diarmaid and Gráinne ". Conception could be prevented if an enemy tied a knot in a handkerchief at the time of marriage ; no child would be born to that couple until the knot was loosed.

A pregnant woman had to avoid meeting a hare, if possible, otherwise her child would be born with a hare-lip *(séanas)* ; this could be prevented, however, if the woman, on meeting the hare, tore the hem of her garment, thereby transferring the blemish to it. A tear in the ear of the hare, if it could be caught, also acted as a preventive. Neither should a pregnant woman enter a graveyard lest she turn her foot on a grave; this would cause her child to be born with a club-foot *(cam reilge)*. She should not remain in a house while a corpse was being placed in the coffin, nor act as sponsor to a bride. If she visited a forge, however, she was always asked to blow the bellows to bring luck to the smith.

Apart from the use of astrology in determining what was in store for persons born under certain planets (as mentioned in folktales), there were many beliefs concerning the time of birth. A child born at night would have the power of seeing ghosts and fairies; but one born on Sunday, at twelve noon or twelve midnight any day, or between twelve noon and twelve midnight would not have this power. Whit Sunday seems, for some reason, to have been regarded as an unlucky time to be born; such a person (called a *Cincíseach*) would either be killed, or else was destined to kill; to avoid the latter fate, a live worm was crushed in such a baby's hand soon after birth. Animals or humans born on May Day were said to be assured of good luck. A child born after its father had died was destined to have special powers (for example, to cure thrush). It was not considered a lucky omen to have three persons born in any house on the same month.

As it was feared that the fairies were always trying to take off newly-born male children, as well as women in child-bed (to nurse them in fairyland), every effort was made to protect both mother and baby from abduction of this kind. Some of the means used were: *Brat Bhríde* (St. Brigid's cloak: a cloth exposed on the eve of her feast), oatmeal (given to the mother when the baby had been born), urine (sprinkled in the room); a piece of iron or a cinder *(aingeal)* concealed in the baby's dress; the tongs placed across the cradle; unsalted butter placed in the baby's mouth; a red ribbon tied across the cradle, and scores of other similar talismans.

Holy water was, of course, in later times regarded as being very efficacious in preserving both mother and child. A charm of which the following is the end, was often invoked to bring about safe delivery of a baby:

A bhean, beir do leanbh,
Mar rug Anna Muire,
Mar rug Muire Dia,
Gan mairtriú, gan daille,
Gan easba coise ná láimhe.

(Woman, bear your child as Anne bore Mary, as Mary bore God, without disfigurement or blindness or lack of foot or hand.)

Despite the vigilant care taken by both the midwife and the people of the house, it was firmly believed that women in child-bed and babies who ailed and wasted away after a while, had been taken by the fairies who had left sickly changelings behind in their stead. This belief was very strong almost down to our own days, but it is never heard of now.

Children who died unbaptised were not buried in consecrated ground in olden times. In many parishes, there were special places, known as *cillínigh* (little graveyards), for such burials, but the little bodies were also laid to rest at boundaries, in the north side of graveyards or in any of several other places. Many stories are told, too, of deceased children returning later to meet the soul of their mother when she too died—the baptised children appeared as strong clear lights, while the unbaptised ones shone weakly.

Traces of the internationally known custom of couvade have been found in Ireland too. By practising this custom,

43

it was hoped to lessen the pangs of childbirth for the mother by transferring some of them to the father. It was usual for a woman who was about to bear a child to wear a waistcoat or some other garment belonging to her husband; or else, the husband had to do some special type of work (such as continuously drawing water from the well) until the baby had been born.

Many other customs and beliefs connected with childbirth and the care of young children must be left undescribed, such as belief in the curative powers of a nursing mother; customs observed when feeding a baby; the various remedies for ailments of babies; rules to be observed concerning the cradle in which all babies were kept in olden times (cradle always borrowed for the first baby); and the beliefs and customs governing the choice of sponsors at baptism.

Marriage too, was a crucial time in human life, and numerous beliefs and customs were brought into play. Only a few can be referred to here. *Pós ar an gcarn aoiligh agus faigh cairdeas Críost i bhfad ó bhaile* (marry among your neighbours, but choose a sponsor for your child from a distance) was a well-known saying. Most rural marriages in Ireland in former times were arranged by matchmakers (*spéicéirí*), who acted on behalf of one or other of the two families involved. It was through them that the dowry, in cash or kind, was arranged—this was very important for the household and farm economy. Arranged marriages are still very common in rural areas, and the system seems to have worked out fairly well down through the centuries. Elopements are now very rare, and the forcible abduction of brides, which was common over a century ago, has ceased altogether. There were, of course, many omens and much divination concerning marriage in general, but these

44

cannot be described here. A few outstanding customs will have to suffice.

When the wedding ceremony was over at the church and the guests set out for the house where the wedding feast *(bainis)* was to be held, it was common in the old days for all the men, with their wives as pillion-riders on horseback, to race against one another from the church to the house. This race was known as " the race for the bottle", the prize being a bottle of whiskey which was placed for the winner near the house. There are accounts of men who, when hard pressed in the race, discarded their wives along the way in an endeavour to win ! Races of this kind were known outside of Ireland also.

Another custom which was prevalent at weddings in many parts of Ireland concerned uninvited guests, who were known as " strawboys" *(geamairí* or *buachaillí tuí)*. They dressed themselves in straw suits, with elaborate headgear (samples can be seen in the National Museum in Dublin), and arrived at the wedding-feast at night. They were generally welcomed, and their leader took the bride out to dance. Then they were given hospitality, and took part in the singing and dancing until morning, still trying to keep their identity a secret. If it happened that, for some reason, their intrusion on the wedding was resented and they were refused hospitality, they had many ways of showing their displeasure. The " strawboy" custom was still quite strong in rural districts in Ireland up to fifty years ago.

Another unusual marriage custom which was practised in Southwest Munster was concerned with Skellig Lists. People in all areas looked forward to being invited to local weddings, especially during Shrove, just before Lent. It often happened then, as now, however, that some marriageable men and women showed no sign, year after year, of "taking the plunge", and were, therefore, unpopular, especially with the younger generation. So, on Shrove Tuesday Night, when the marriage season was over for a while, much mischief was done to the houses and farms of bachelors and spinsters: the walls of the houses might be daubed, the chimney stuffed, the gates taken off their hinges, the cows loosed from the byre, the wheels taken off the cart and so on. Bottles, from which the bases had been removed, were also used as trumpets and were blown near the unpopular houses, summoning the unmarried people to travel to the Skelligs, rocks off the Kerry coast. It is possible that in olden times, when monks lived on these inhospitable rocks, the date of Easter was later there than even on the mainland, where it was certainly later than on the continent of Europe, after the calendar had been changed. If this was so, it could have meant that Lent began later on the Skelligs than elsewhere, and consequently marriages could still be celebrated there when they were no longer permissible on the mainland. As well as this token summoning of bachelors and spinsters to set out for the Skelligs (which custom continued for centuries after the monastic settlement there had been deserted), ballads of a rather crude type, known as Skellig Lists, were composed in many southwestern districts of Ireland, describing how the most incongruous pairs from each parish arrived at the distant rocks to be married. I remember well how these songs were still being made in my native parish in South Kerry up to 1920. Crofton Croker, in *Popular Songs of Ireland*, enumerates the many such "lists" which were published in ballad form in Cork in the early eighteenth century. The custom seems to have died out completely now.

In the days before medical knowledge became scientifically grounded, people everywhere throughout the world looked upon various illnesses as having been caused not so much by bodily weaknesses or contagion, as by malignant unknown powers. " Blasts " and " fairy strokes " *(poic sí)* were commonly spoken of when it was thought that the fairies had stricken somebody whom they wished to take off into their own world. If somebody who had spoken of seeing a ghost took to his bed and died soon afterwards, it was believed that the ghost had taken him off to the other world. Hence the many precautions taken to ward off illness and the inimical effects of evil **powers**, as well as the attempts to protect newly-born babies and their mothers.

As regards sickness itself, *bloscadh an Domhnaigh* (an improvement in the patient's condition on Sunday) was, for some reason, regarded as an ill-omen. *Dhá dtrian galar na hoíche* (a patient is doubly ill at night) was another popular saying, which may have had some basis in fact. That the doctor was sent for only as a last resort is evidenced by the proverb *dearbhráthair don Bhás fios a chur ar an dochtúir* (sending for the doctor is brother to Death). It was considered wrong to visit a sick person when one was returning from a funeral, or to allow milk or fire out of a house in which somebody was ill. Every effort was made to keep the fire well-stoked at such a time—the life of the fire being in some way symbolic of the life of the patient.

When a person was seriously ill, it was to be expected that the immediate relatives would be " on edge " and would take special notice of normal things and regard them as omens for good or ill. For example : if a bird perched on the window-sill of the sick-room, if a dog howled outside at night, if a raven or scaldcrow was seen flying over the house, or if some natural sound was heard, which resembled wailing and was identified as the banshee (a fairy woman who was supposed to cry when members of certain families were dying)—all of these happenings, and many others, were looked upon as sure signs of approaching death. Coincidence, as well as faulty interpretation of natural occurrences at this critical time, gave rise to many omens being taken for certainties.

Death was the supreme crisis in human affairs. Great though its impact on the surviving relatives is today, it must have been still greater in olden times. An apocryphal story told in Ireland illustrates this. When Cain had killed Abel, he ran away, and the body was found by the relatives of both men. They had never seen a dead body before, as Abel is said to have been the first human being to die, so they gathered around the body, trying to help. They could not understand why Abel did not speak to them. Then, according to the story, an angel came to them and explained that Abel was dead as far as this world was concerned, and told them to dig a grave of certain dimensions and place him in it. Today as then, the mystery of death tends to confound our human understanding and gives us a feeling of helplessness.

In early times, Death seems to have been personified in a different way from the modern artistic conception of a skeletal man holding a scythe which cuts everybody down at some stage. Early literature mentions a female goddess or mythical being named Morrigan, who haunted the battlefields. Later times have given us the *badhb* ("bow") or scaldcrow as symbolising Death; this is illustrated in the story of the dying Cúchulainn on whose shoulder, at the moment of his death, there perched a bird to claim his life (the Sheppard

PATTERN DAY AT A HOLY WELL

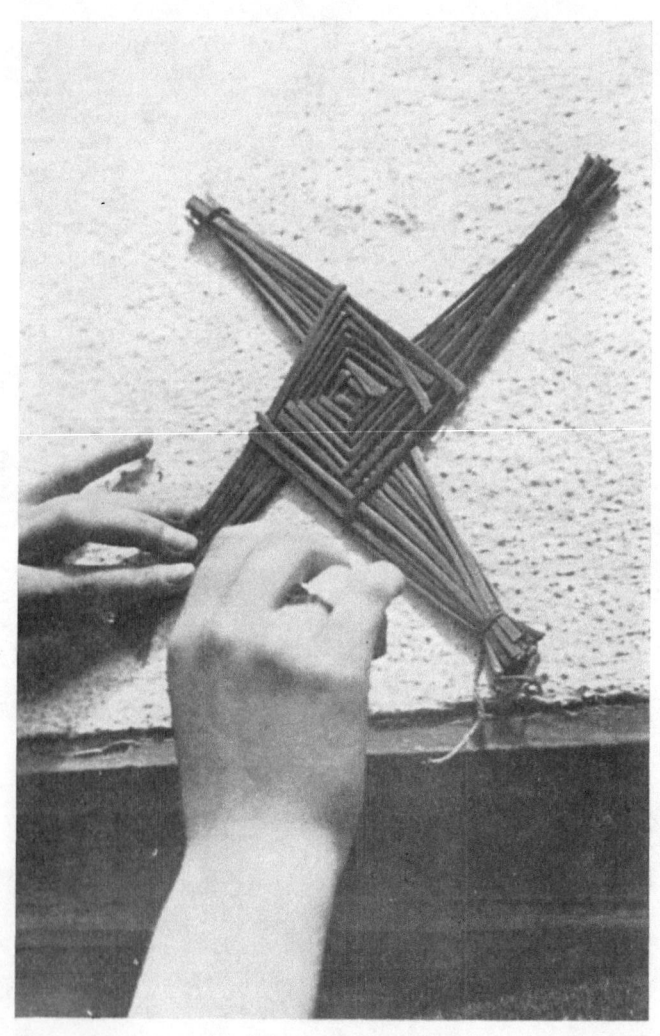

SAINT BRIGID'S CROSS

statue in the General Post Office in Dublin graphically depicts this).

The continuation of some kind of existence by the dead after they had departed this life was believed in by all peoples, even before the coming of Christianity. Where this kingdom of the dead lay was, of course, the subject of much speculation. In Ireland, a mythical figure referred to as Donn Fírinne was thought to rule over the dead, and a hill in Co. Limerick called Cnoc Fírinne was said to be his abode. Some peoples placed the dead in islands (*Toteninseln*—isles of the dead) off their coast, and Kuno Meyer has hinted at the rocks off the mouth of Kenmare Bay (Bull, Cow and Calf), one of which was known as Tigh Dhoinn (the house of Donn), as being associated with this belief in Ireland. Such ancient beliefs were, of their nature, never very clearly defined and have become still more blurred through the passage of time.

When a person was dying, every effort of the relatives seems to have been intended in early times (as still evidenced by extant folk belief) to ease the passage of the soul, or whatever it was, and make the parting easier. Doors and windows were opened—in some countries, including Ireland, a special hole was formerly made in the wall or thatched roof to allow the spirit to escape. In Ireland too, as in other lands, the dying person was sometimes taken from the bed and placed on straw on the floor to die, lest the feather of some wild bird in the tick might prolong the struggle.

An international story of an aetiological character, which is found in Ireland, relates that foreknowledge of the time of death was finally withdrawn from human beings, after they had been shown to be improvident regarding the welfare of those who survived them. The hour of death was popularly associated with the fall of the tide. The legend of the foxes which were said to gather around Gormanston Castle in Co. Meath when a member of the family was dying is well known—one of the many omens observed at such a crucial point of human life. *Bás Aoine, adhlacadh Shathairn, agus guí an phobail Dé Domhnaigh* (death on Friday, burial on Saturday and Sunday remembrance in church prayers) is evidently a Christian wish. It was thought lucky to die during the Twelve Days of Christmas, as the gates of Heaven were said to stand open during that period. In olden times, the occurrence of death was signalled to the neighbours by burning outside the house a bundle of straw or the straw bed of the deceased. The clock was usually stopped at the moment of death, and mirrors were veiled. It was customary too to tell the sad news to the bees, if a hive were kept, and a crêpe was placed on it.

There were so many customs observed in connection with death that only a few can be mentioned or described here. The corpse was laid out for the wake by local women and was shaved by some neighbour, if necessary. In recent times it has been laid out in a habit—black for elderly persons some years ago, but nowadays more generally brown. A crucifix was placed in the hands, and the bed or table on which the body lay was hung on three sides and overhead with white sheets. Lighted candles stood on a table nearby for the duration of the wake. It was a strict traditional rule that, at no time during the wake, should the corpse be left alone; if it were waked in a room off the kitchen or upstairs (in modern houses), some people, usually women, sat in relays nearby.

Neighbours and relatives visited the wake-house either by day or night, as was convenient; old people generally did so in the daytime. Young children in the house were sent to relatives or friends for the duration of the wake. In olden times, wakes lasted for two nights, the second one bringing the largest gathering of sympathisers from far and near. When one entered the house, one went directly to the place where the body was laid out, knelt down and prayed for the soul of the deceased, and then offered sympathy to the relatives who might be sitting or standing nearby, before taking one's place inside the house (or outside, in fine weather) among those assembled. Food and drink, as well as pipes, tobacco and snuff were offered to all and were generally accepted, according to traditional usage. The Rosary was recited at Catholic wakes about midnight, after which many people left for their homes.

In olden times and down almost to the beginning of the present century, wakes were merry occasions over the greater part of Ireland, especially if the deceased were an old person. Stories were told; songs were sung; music was played for dancing; and hundreds of games were played " to pass away the night and to keep the people awake ". As I have described elsewhere this merry aspect of Irish (and foreign) wakes in former times, there is no need to do so here. No disrespect for the dead or for the relatives was intended by this sometimes unruly and boisterous behaviour in the presence of the dead. It would seem to have had its origin in ancient times when fear of the dead was very strong among primitive peoples everywhere. They feared that the dead were envious of the living who had survived them and that they were anxious to take revenge on those who succeeded to their property. Hence, every effort was made to assure the dead one of their sympathy and friendship; he was still one of them, so to speak, while the wake lasted, and this was shown by the feasting, drinking and amusements which took place in his honour. The Church in Europe had, since the early centuries of Christianity, endeavoured to end abuses which resulted from wake festivities; so too, in Ireland, many Catholic Synods condemned them, and it was only finally, almost in our own day, when it was ordered that the corpse be taken to the church on the evening before the interment, that wake amusements came to an end. Although the wake, as an institution, has died out over the greater part of Europe for several decades, it still continues in a subdued and decorous form in Ireland.

Much traditional ritual was associated with the coffin in which the body was placed before it left the house. It was usually made by some carpenter in an adjoining outhouse in the old days; the exact age of the dead, though known, was never inscribed on the breastplate. Goods (money, food, weapons, extra clothes, holy water, etc.) were formerly placed in the coffin for the use of the deceased. This was a world-wide custom; it is from paintings of these goods on the walls of ancient Egyptian tombs that we derive our main knowledge of the early death customs and beliefs of that country. In penal times, when Catholic priests were not allowed by law to attend funerals in graveyards, they blessed some clay at the house, and this was put into the coffin or grave—this custom was a Christian one, of course, and had no connection with the older one of grave-goods.

When the coffin was taken out from the house, it was placed for a few moments on chairs, which were immediately knocked down after the coffin had been raised on to the shoulders of the bearers. Four men of the same surname as the deceased bore the coffin, in relays, to the graveyard or, if a cart or hearse were used, placed it on that. Hundreds of tabus and aspects of ritual were connected with the funeral too: its route to the graveyard (*gach timpal le sochraid*: no shortcut for a funeral), its occasional stops; attendance at funerals and the dress worn; double funerals at graveyards (rivalry as to which would be first); unusual funerals. Not one book but many could be written about all of these aspects of death. So too with regard to customs and beliefs associated with graveyards in general and some in particular, e.g., supernatural funerals at night bring bodies from afar to the *teampoll dúchais* (family graveyard); the arrival of the funeral at the graveyard and the route taken to the open grave; the many customs and beliefs connected with the digging of the grave (spade and shovel crossed over the empty grave) and the burial itself, together with the blessing and prayers of the priest. Finally, much could be written about " body-snatchers " who, in the early days of medical knowledge, stole newly-buried corpses from graves and sold them for experimental purposes to doctors (the watch-towers at the corners of Glasnevin Cemetery in Dublin are reminders of this).

Not only was food put outside the house for the dead for some time after their burial, but it was also customary, especially in the south-west of Ireland, for a near relative of the dead man or woman to wear a new suit or dress on behalf of the dead person at Mass for three Sundays after the funeral. Much ritual was associated with this strange custom, with its superficial clothing of Christian observance, and hundreds of stories were told of the dead who returned to complain that the custom had not been observed at all or only carelessly carried out. When this custom was breaking down in some areas, the clothes for the deceased were not worn at Mass but rather taken there in a parcel. It is still fully practised in some parishes however.

A final word or two about the practice of keening (lamenting for) the dead. It was but natural that the near relatives would cry over the dead body as soon as it had been laid out, and again during the wake when distant relations arrived. In addition to this heartfelt expression of sorrow, there was added, however, the custom of hiring men and women, whose profession it was to compose eulogies over the dead to the accompaniment of loud, artificial wailing. This was a widespread European practice in olden times and was general in Ireland down to almost the end of the last century, until it was finally stamped out by the clergy. Poets too, were accustomed to compose *caointe* or *mairbhní* (dirges) in memory of persons who had died tragically or whose death was regarded as a great loss. Many of these have survived in folk poetry, but the custom has now become almost extinct in Ireland.

One of the richest and strongest aspects of folk belief was that which was concerned with the so-called return of the dead from beyond the grave for various reasons. The belief in ghosts is a typical example of this. Here it is possible only to mention briefly some of the reasons given for the supposed return of the dead : to revisit the old home or family (especially when a dead mother came in the dead of night to watch over her orphan children) ; to give help of some kind to the living, or else to seek prayers or help (if the soul were in Purgatory), or to complain of some neglected traditional observance; to fulfil a promise or accept an invitation to return (this is the theme of some folktales) ; to meet the newly dead and convey

54

them to the other world; to give warnings about impending disasters; to seek revenge for some wrong, and so on. Students of ancient religious beliefs can find abundant information in stories about the return of the dead, not only in Ireland but elsewhere.

VI. HEALING THE SICK

IN OLDEN TIMES as well as today, primitive peoples the world over had little, if any, understanding of the composition and functioning of the human body. Indeed, even in our own so-called enlightened days, medical men are still trying to cope with hundreds of problems in the field of medicine. It is not to be wondered at, therefore, that our ancient ancestors had ideas about the human body and its maladies which seem very strange to us. Most ailments were attributed to the action of unfriendly powers: evil spirits, fairies, ghosts and so on. Man's main weapon against them was magic, and his efforts gave him comfort, even if they did not always bring relief.

Hippocrates, the Greek "father of medicine", who lived in the fifth century, B.C., and his numerous successors tried in their various ways to understand the human body and its illnesses. Still, so slow was the progress made, that even in the seventeenth century a native of the African forests had about the same chances of survival from disease as any European farmer. When surgery and medical knowledge progressed in later times, folk techniques in dealing with disease and sickness were branded as quackery and were forbidden by law in many countries. Still, the old, traditional remedies lived on among the common people, who were uninfluenced by book-learning and were out of reach of the relatively few doctors of the time.

The simples and other "cures" of the countryside were looked upon as both ridiculous and dangerous until fairly recent times, when medical men discovered that at least some items of folk medicine had a sound and rational basis. This came about through the search for new medicines. Salicyl, made from the bark of some types of willow, was found to have been used by primitive peoples for hundreds, if not thousands, of years as a remedy for rheumatism. It is now a standard medical therapeutic. The Hottentots long ago discovered aspirin. The people in the Amazon jungle used curare against their enemies—it is now a valuable drug in modern operating theatres. The Incas gave us knowledge of cocaine and quinine. So too, the extract of the foxglove plant, digitalin, had been used traditionally in Ireland and elsewhere as a remedy for heart ailments. Even penicillin, which was accidentally discovered by Sir Alexander Fleming in recent years, was used in Ireland as a popular cure for septic wounds long before that; country people kept a loaf of white bread or a piece of bacon in a damp part of the house and applied the mould which grew on them to sores which were slow to heal.

Besides these now popular medical remedies, many other ancient ones could be listed from the pharmacopeia of the common people, who also had traditional knowledge of the value of plasters and compresses, hot baths and other medicaments. Even surgery seems to have been attempted in olden times, as witness the story of the brain-ball in Conor mac Nessa's head and the silver hand of Nuada Lámh-airgid. The drawing of blood, as a remedy for certain illnesses, has a long history; scarification and blood-letting *(cuisleoireacht)* were well-known in Ireland, as was the international use of leeches, which were on sale in this country at a shilling each in 1836.

It has been estimated, from present-day knowledge, that about twenty-five per cent of old-time medicaments were rationally based and as effective as they are today in modern medicine. It is possible that the figure will increase as further study of folk remedies is made from the purely medical point of view. The extensive field of herbal recipes *(luibheanna leighis)* has hardly been explored at all by medical scientists. It is probable that at least some hundreds of the many thousand so-called curative herbs used by our ancestors in Ireland and elsewhere will be found to contain useful drugs or other ingredients.

It is curious to discover that specialists in herbal medicine in all countries, while being useful and respected members of their communities, seem to have been the lowest grade of medicine-men. This will be better understood when we come to consider the attitude of primitive man everywhere towards sickness' and disease, an attitude which is completely foreign to the rational world in which we live. The straight-forward cure of some ailment by the simple application of a plaster or other remedy did not impress our ancestors half so much as the ritual carried out by the local " wise " man or woman to effect a cure. The ceremonial curing of a com-plaint, by the recitation of an often corrupt spell or charm *(ortha)*, as well as by complicated acts and gestures, not only reassured the patient but also his relatives and people generally. The patient's faith in the efficacy of the cure was activated by the complicated ritual of the " doctor ", and he felt better as a result. This has been proved to be the case in modern medicine too. The faith of the average patient in the power of medicine is so great that improvement, even recovery, can result even though the medicine itself is intrinsically ineffective. Experiments in the United States have shown that useless tablets given to some patients in a test worked just as well as efficient ones on others. Healing through faith in the power of the healer and his medicine is a very old phenomenon.

The beliefs and customs associated with folk medicine in Ireland are very numerous. Illnesses might be caused by evil neighbours (through looks, curses or wishes) or by fairies (*poc sí*—"fairy stroke") or inimical spirits, just as often as they might arise through some bodily weakness or infection. Precautions against illness included going around the mid-summer bonfire thrice, abstaining from meat on St. Stephen's Day, taking three meals of nettles in May, the possession of a *brat Bhríde* (St. Brigid's cloak), drinking blessed Easter water on Easter Sunday, and many others. The diagnosis of complaints took such strange forms as weighing or measuring the patient, scanning the heavens and observing the behaviour of particular plants.

In the treatment of ailments, magic necessarily played a prominent part. It was believed that diseases could be transferred to objects (I have already referred to the banishment of warts in this connection) or to other persons; this belief was widespread throughout the Roman Empire. Forge-water (probably because of its association with iron) and water from a triple boundary were much in vogue as remedies. So too were relics of saints; even lying in the supposed tomb or bed of a saint was expected to bring relief. Cupping to raise the fallen *cléithín* (breastbone), the use of sweat-houses and hot baths, as well as hundreds of other traditional recipes, were normal parts of old-time medicine, as practised. Passing the patient through an opening, by which he was supposed to leave his ailment behind at the other side, was commonly carried out; I have seen dozens of pilgrims to St. Declan's well at Ardmore, Co. Waterford, crawl laboriously through an opening under a stone on the nearby strand to rid themselves of rheumatism—this stone was variously said to have carried the saint's forgotten Mass-book or bell across the sea after him, or else to have indicated to him where he should land and build his church. Children were similarly pushed through some kinds of openings (clefts in trees and so on) to cure rickets.

While many of the so-called medical cures were handed down traditionally (the practice of medicine was hereditary in some families), others came from old-time medical books. Still, many practitioners of healing were thought to have received their powers from higher sources. Posthumous children (because of the unusual circumstances of their birth), the seventh son or seventh son of a seventh son (with no daughter intervening), persons with certain surnames, silenced priests, blacksmiths and many others were considered as having special medical powers. Charm-setters (persons who knew traditional charms) were much in vogue as healers, and great mystery surrounded the application of these verbal cures. "Wise" men and women were often among this latter class. By using whatever knowledge they had inherited and allying it with shrewd observation and commonsense, as well as a constructive imagination, they were able to impress their neighbours not only with their medical skill, but also with their knowledge of faraway events (supposedly got through their association with the fairies) and their ability to give sound advice beyond the powers of others. In their own day, all of these " doctors " and many others whom I have not enumerated filled a very useful social function, although their activities would be looked upon askance in our less sympathetic days.

VII. FESTIVAL, PATTERN AND PILGRIMAGE

A VERY LARGE body of custom and belief centred upon the various festivals, prechristian and Christian, which occurred each year. Only the main ones can be included here.

I happened to be visiting a family in Dublin about thirty years ago. It was New Year's Eve and, as the bells of the city rang out to welcome in the New Year, I was led outside the door by the man of the house and invited to come in again. This was, I was informed, because I was dark-haired, and would thus bring luck to the house for the ensuing year. New Year's Day was referred to in Irish as either *Lá Coille* (Kalends Day) or *Lá na nIarsmaí* (The day of New Year gifts), the latter being explained by the custom of young people, boys and girls, going from house to house on that day asking for gifts of money or kind. This custom must have come in at a rather late period, because in olden times nobody would risk losing his luck for the year by giving away money on that day; neither would milk be given away; nor would even the ashes or the floor-sweepings be put out. Digging a grave or burying somebody was also avoided on that day.

The Twelve Days of Christmas ended on January 6 (popularly knows as Small Christmas or *Nollaig na mBan* : Women's Christmas, as distinct from the main feast, *Nollaig na bhFear :* Men's Christmas). The Christmas holly was taken down and burned at this time, and twelve candles were lighted in homes in honour of the Twelve Apostles; the first candle to die out was looked upon as an omen that the person who had lighted it would be the first of the family to die. The Eve of the Feast was known as *Oíche na dTrí*

Rithe (The Night of the Three Kings), and was said to correspond with the wedding feast of Cana. A popular Irish saying was:

> *Oíche na dTrí Rithe*
> *Deintear fíon den uisce,*
> *Síoda den triopall*
> *Agus ór den ghrean.*

(On the Night of the Three Kings, water becomes wine, clusters of rushes become silk, and the sand becomes gold.)

St. Brigid's Feast (February 1) was originally an important prechristian festival, occurring as it did at the time of the start of agricultural work. For some reason which is not clear, people would perform no work which involved turning or twisting on that day, such as spinning, digging, ploughing or using a wheel: *bíonn Lá 'le Bríde ina shaoire ar chasaíbh* (St. Brigid's Day is free from twistings.) Shellfish was brought into houses near the sea and put in the four corners of the floor to invoke plenty of fish for the rest of the year. Young boys (*Brídeoga :* " Biddies") went from door to door carrying a churndash dressed as a woman and asked for some gift. Rushes or straw were left outside the house on the Eve of the Feast, and at nightfall a young girl went out, brought the bundle to the door, and knocked, asking in the name of Brigid to be admitted. When this was done, crosses (of various designs and materials, according to different districts) were woven or otherwise made, to the accompaniment of a traditional prayer. A meal was then taken, and the crosses were placed both in the inner side of the thatched roof and in the outhouses to invoke protection for the family and livestock. It was said that, as one cross was placed in the roof each year, the age of many old houses in Ireland could be reckoned by the number of crosses. A girdle *(crios)* was also woven of straw or rushes that evening, and both the members of the family and the cows passed through it for protection against illness. A cloth, known as *brat Bhríde* (Brigid's cloak) was left in the open that night and was then preserved for the healing powers it was said to have acquired. Another ancient custom was the throwing of a sheaf of oats or a cake of bread against the doorstep that evening to " drive away hunger " and to ensure a supply of food for the family during the year.

St. Patrick's Day fell on March 17 : *Ní díri bradán fearna i lár na caise ná Lá 'le Pádraig i lár an Earraigh* (as the sturgeon or salmon swims exactly in mid-stream, so does St. Patrick's Day fall exactly in mid-Spring). It was jocosely said that on that day the cold stone which had been placed in the water at Hallowe'en was again removed. Weather was expected to improve : every other day fine after St. Brigid's Day, every day fine after his own Feast, St. Patrick is said to have promised. People endeavoured to sow their grain as near to this Feast as possible. The old men celebrated it by going together to the publichouse to drink " *pota Phádraic* " (St. Patrick's pot). Crosses in rosette form were made of coloured ribbons and worn on the breast ; this custom appears to be of comparatively recent origin. A much older one would seem to be that which took the following form : the father of the family marked the arm of himself and each member of the family with a cross made with a charred stick " in the name of the Father and of the Son and of the Holy Ghost ". Our earliest literary reference to the wearing of shamrock on St. Patrick's Day is for the year 1681, so the custom may not be a very old one. It may be said too that it appears as if the legend of the use by St. Patrick of the shamrock to explain the Trinity is of rather recent vintage (no reference earlier than the year 1727).

The festivals of the Virgin Mary in Spring (March 25) and in Autumn (August 15) were not important, so far as the popular lore attached to them is concerned. Fishermen did not put to sea on the eve of the first-named feast. It was considered a bad omen if it coincided with Easter Sunday (*díol do bhó agus ceannaigh lón :* if it happens, sell your cow and buy food). People tried, if possible, to start the reaping of their grain-crops around the August festival. Many patterns (local festivals) took place on both feasts, and rounds were made at holy wells popularly dedicated to Our Lady.

Shrovetide has already been referred to as a very popular time for weddings, and the last night of it was an occasion for feasting. Meat, if available, was eaten that night, and a boiled piece of it, known as *Tadhg an Gheimhridh* (" Tim the Winter ") was hung on a spike in the kitchen for the duration of Lent, which began next day. Pancakes, baked in some areas over the blazing Christmas holly, were a popular food on Shrove Tuesday Night.

Lent was a much more strict period of fast and abstinence in olden times that it is now (the flesh of barnacle geese, said to have the nature of fish, was eaten in some areas, however). " *Bia bocht* " (poor fare) was the general diet. On Ash Wednesday people were wont to take some turf-ashes to the church to be blessed and some of it was sprinkled over the house and land. Palm Sunday was known as *Domhnach na Slat* from the sprigs of yew worn as palm, and on that day children started to collect eggs from the neighbours for their Easter Sunday feast. Many customs and tabus centred around Good Friday : no meat should be hung on a nail that day,

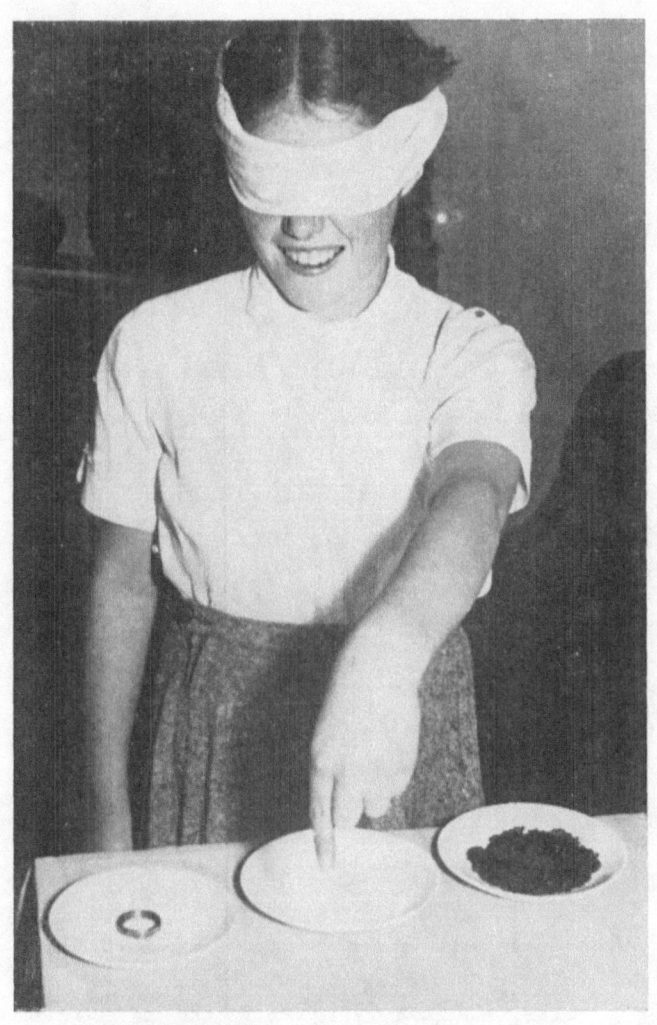

MARRIAGE DIVINATION AT HALLOWE'EN

HUNTING THE WREN ON SAINT STEPHEN'S DAY

nor should any nail be driven, or wood burned; no blood should be shed on that day, when the sun was said to grow darker after noon; no milk was drunk; cakes baked on that day had the Sign of the Cross marked on them; women and girls allowed their hair to hang loose. It was supposed to be lucky to plant some seed potatoes that day, and anybody who had his hair cut would be free from headaches for a year. Eggs were the most popular food on Easter Sunday—meat was also eaten, but it was far less plentiful in olden times than it is now. Blessed Easter water was drunk, and some of it was sprinkled on the fields. The shells of used eggs were used to decorate the May-bush in those areas of Ireland where such bushes were erected—it does not seem to have been a native Irish custom at all. Whitsuntide was a dangerous time for bathing: " *Tá stiúradh ag an gCincís ar an bhfaraige*" (Whitsuntide has control of the sea).

To judge by the hundreds of customs and beliefs which were associated with May Day, it must have been the most important annual festival in ancient Ireland. Both the eve of May Day and the day itself were important as signifying the start of Summer and the coming in of the milk and butter produce which were staple foods for our forefathers. Almost every custom and belief associated with them seems to have sprung from the need people felt to protect their livestock and preserve their luck at this crucial time.

Summer was welcomed in by the carrying of green branches and flowers into the house or strewing them around the doors and windows. " *Thugamar féin an Samhradh linn* " (We have brought the Summer with us) is the name of an Irish song which was associated with this custom, which is still popular in many rural districts.

A description of the precautions taken to protect the live stock at that time of year would fill a large volume. Holy water was, of course, sprinkled on the byre and cows in later times, but older precautions involved the recitation of charms, driving the cattle between blazing bonfires, and the tying of rings of rowan on the animals' tails (red ribbons were attached to the manes and harness of horses, too). Reference has already been made to the means traditionally adopted to protect the cows, the milk, and the churn, and all of these were more important than ever at Maytime, when evilly-disposed persons would try to steal a whole year's " profit " by magic. So people guarded their wells on May Eve and May Morn, as it was believed that they were intimately connected with the family's prosperity. By bailing a neighbour's well-water in the direction of her own home or by drawing a rope or cloth over the dew on a neighbour's grass on May Morn, while chanting " Come all to me ! " a hag was supposed to be able to steal the potential produce of milk and butter for herself. As a counter to this, salt and holy water were put into the well. I have already described how no coal of fire would be allowed out of a house while churning was in progress. Similarly, people did not light their fires early on May Day as a further precaution. In olden times, and still in some districts, people did not work at all on May Day.

Being associated with a *ceann féile* (chief festival), May Eve and May Day were supposed to be times of greater than usual activity among supernatural beings. Every *lios* (" fairy fort ") in Ireland was said to be open that night, and their inhabitants moved abroad in great numbers, often changing their residence at that time. Thus, people were loth to be out late on May Eve, and many stories were told of the strange experiences of those who took the risk. Other strange things were said to happen too: enchanted riders like Donal O'Donoghue rode on a white horse, with silver shoes, over the Lakes of Killarney; bewitched rocks moved from place to place; and mermaids were often seen. Like all chief festivals, May Eve was a great time for attempts at divining the future, but these cannot be listed here.

Owing to the change in the calendar, most of the customs and beliefs which were attached to Old May Day (now May 11) came to be transferred to the new date. They are now becoming only a memory, except in some areas where the old ways of thought still hold sway.

The Feast of St. John (June 24) seems to have been celebrated by the church in an attempt to christianise the old festival of midsummer, which occurred about that time. The lighting of bonfires, which is still carried out in many areas in Ireland, is a very ancient custom and was once found all over the world. Many attempts have been made to interpret the minds of the early peoples who started the custom—one theory was that people lit the fires to boost the strength of the sun, which, they knew by experience, would wane from that day onwards. We may never know the real explanation, if there was only one. It does not matter. In Ireland, village inhabitants often joined together in lighting a huge fire; but in scattered farms, each owner lit his own bonfire and ended by throwing some of the blazing bushes into his crops for luck. As at May Eve, cattle were driven between two such fires to protect them from harm of various kinds. Diseases were said to grow less as each *ceann féile* approached; still people also tried to help themselves and improve their health by bathing on midsummer eve and drinking the boiled juice of St. John's weed. The reaping hook was symbolically placed among the unripe corn on that evening too. As on May Eve, fairies and spirits were active then also.

Bonfires again blazed on the Feast of SS. Peter and Paul (June 29) and people looked forward to the day being fine as an augury of a good harvest:

Lá 'le Póil má fhónann grian go geal,
Beidh grán go leor, 's gach sórt sa bhliain go maith.

(If the sun shines brightly on St. Paul's Day, plenty of grain and all good things are assured for the year). St. Swithin's Day in July was said to commemorate the day on which the Deluge began, and rain on that day was a bad omen for the ensuing forty days.

The Feast of Lughnasa was celebrated either at the end of July or early in August. As Máire Mac Neill has shown in her monumental study of this ancient Celtic festival, it was celebrated to welcome in the first fruits of the harvest. It was popularly known by scores of local names, ranging from Domhnach Chrom Dubh (Crom Dubh's Sunday), Donagh Sunday, Bilberry Sunday, Fraughan Sunday, Garland (Garlic) Sunday, Mountain (Rock) Sunday, Domhnach na bhFear (The Men's Sunday) and many others to the Sunday of the New Potatoes. The feast was celebrated on either the last Sunday in July or the first Sunday in August, whichever fell closest to the first of August. It is now best known as the Sunday on which the annual pilgrimage is made to Croagh Patrick in Co. Mayo, but scores at least of local pilgrimages, of a social rather than a religious character, were made formerly on that day to hills throughout the country, where the day was spent in sports, picking whortle-berries, and other amusements. The first fruits of the harvest, in the form of wild berries, were eaten on that day, as later were the first new potatoes of that year's crop. People also assembled at certain lakes and rivers on that festival, and horses and cattle were set to swim in the water. Many wells were also meeting-places for the people on that day, and fairs (such as Puck Fair in Killorglin, in Kerry, and many others) were also associated with the festival of Lughnasa.

People tried to have their harvest of grain-crops secured by the time the Feast of St. Bartholomew (August 24) came around. Flails for threshing were then got ready. High winds were also expected at that time, which were jocosely explained as being caused by the saint wielding his own flail.

St. Michael (the Archangel) was commemorated by the feast of Michaelmas in September. "Summer is Summer until Michaelmas" was a common saying. Sickness was expected to grow less at the approach of the festival. An animal (sheep) or bird (goose) was ceremonially killed and eaten in the saint's honour; in many districts some of the blood was rubbed to the doors. As well as this kind of sacrificial slaying, this was the period of the year when most farmers killed a beef for winter food, and the slaying also served to lessen the number of livestock they would have to feed during the winter. As on some other festivals, fishermen would not go to sea on the eve of the Feast.

As Hallowe'en corresponds with an ancient Feast of the Dead, it was to be expected that much of its lore would be concerned with the dead, the fairies and spirits in general. All "fairy forts" were said to be open on the eve of the festival, and their occupants were believed to change their residence from one centre to another on that night; it was a dangerous night for people to be out of doors, it was said, for fear of "fairy stroke" or abduction. Houses were got ready for any deceased relatives who might visit the old home during the night, and food was laid out for them. Candles were lighted in windows too. Colcannon was a popular dish at the evening meal, as were nuts, and many games were played and divinatory acts performed afterwards. The food supply for the winter being very important, hunger and famine were symbolically banished by throwing a cake of bread against the door. As the weather was expected to deteriorate from that date on ("when the cold stone was put into the water"), sheep were brought to the lowlands from the higher grazing-grounds, and other farm livestock were housed for the winter. This was the time, too, for the payment of "gales" or "half-gales" of rent to the landlord, and servants who had been hired for the summer and harvest work were allowed to go.

"*Naoi n-oíche agus oíche gan áireamh*
Ó Oíche Shamhna go hOíche 'l Mártain."

(Nine nights and a night uncounted from Hallowe'en to the Eve of the Feast of St. Martin.) The Irish commemoration of the saint (who was not an Irishman) was on November 11, and it seems that it was meant to christianise an ancient prechristian festival. As on the feast of St. Brigid, no action should be performed on St. Martin's Day which involved twisting or turning: no spinning, no use of wheels, no fishing (which involved the turning of boats), and, above all, no grinding of corn in mills or by quern-stones. In Ireland, many mills still remain idle on that day. The legend to explain this tabu tells that St. Martin was ground to death in a mill—hence the prohibition against milling on his feast-day. As no such death appears historically to have been the fate of any Christian saint named Martin, it is possible that we have here

70

an echo of a much earlier belief. It may be that, as people in the Middle East of old believed that the god Tammuz, who had given them the harvest, was being ground to death along with the corn between the quern-stones, and let down their hair and wept, so too in Ireland Martin, the Christian saint, replaced some pagan deity who was associated with the grinding of the harvest. In any case, as at the earlier Feast of Michaelmas, a bird or animal was sacrificed on the eve of the Feast of St. Martin with much traditional ritual, and some of the blood was placed on the foreheads of members of the family and on the doors (possibly, as in the case of the Holy Innocents, to signify that the sacrifice had been carried out). The flesh was eaten at a ceremonial feast next day. Like some of the other chief festivals, the customs and beliefs in this case have roots which go deep down into prehistory and the early beliefs of our ancestors. In Ireland, this sacrificial shedding of blood was practically unknown in the south-west and north-east.

And so we come to the great Feast of Christmas and the end of the year. Christmas, like Hallowe'en, was also an ancient time for commemorating the dead and approximated to the winter solstice. Holly, as a means of decorating the house, is now joined by commercially-produced streamers and tinsel; and the Christmas tree, still absent in simple traditional country homes, has come from central Europe to invade our cities and towns. One of the most beautiful of our old Irish customs is that of lighting one large candle in the kitchen window on Christmas Eve, as well as a smaller one in each of the other windows of the house. This was said to be in honour of the Holy Family who sought shelter on that night long ago, and the lights also served as a beacon for lonely and homeless wayfarers. The placing of a large log *(bloc na Nollag)* at the side of the open hearth in Irish homes for the Twelve Days of Christmas had a possible counterpart in the *tinte éigin* ("need fires") custom in Gaelic Scotland. The religious observance of Christmas is, of course, the principal expression of the Feast in present-day Ireland, as it has been down through the centuries.

There is no trace that I know of in Irish tradition of the European celebration of the Feast of St. Stephen (December 26) by horse-riding around castles and such; the fact that he is regarded as the patron of horses does not seem to have left any mark in this country. The day was, instead, popularly observed by "wren-boys", groups of boys or young men who went from door to door carrying a holly bush, on which was either a dead wren or something to represent the bird. They sang a song which began:

"The wren, the wren, the king of all birds,
St. Stephen's Day was caught in the furze;
Although he is little, his family is great,
So rise up, landlady, and give us a treat;
Bottles of whiskey and bottles of beer,
And I wish you all a happy New Year."

When the song had ended (often in the grey dawn, as rival groups tried to be first in their visit to each house), they would be given some money. All wore masks or some other facial and bodily disguise, in the traditional manner of carnival singers the world over. This custom is still strong in some areas, but has died out almost completely in others. As already mentioned, people in many districts still abstain from meat on St. Stephen's Day; the reason popularly given for this is that, when plague threatened the parish in olden times, the people prayed to St. Stephen to save them—which he did—and ever since they have thanked him in this way. It is possible too that, since meat was a comparative rarity in olden times, people ate so much of it on Christmas Day that they did not feel like eating more next day.

Lá na Leanbh (Children's Day : Feast of the Holy Innocents) fell on December 28 and, for some unknown reason, was known also as *Lá Crosta na Bliana* (" The Cross Day of the Year "). The word " cross " *(crosadh)* here signifies prohibition : people would not begin any kind of work on that day or dig a grave or get married.

New Year's Eve, the last night of the old year, was known as *Oíche Chinn Bhliana* (Year's End Night) and *Oíche na Coda Móire* (The Night of the Great Feast). Candles were again lighted in the windows and special food was eaten. It was a night which was associated with the dead too, and both they and absent members of families were remembered in the family rosary. As the New Year, with its many uncertainties, was near at hand, a cake of bread was again dashed against the door to banish the danger of hunger, and the rise or fall of rivers was observed to foretell whether prices would correspond during the ensuing year. There was no general traditional custom of bidding goodbye to the old year and welcoming in the new one, which is now internationally observed in modern times.

Patterns and Pilgrimages

As well as observing the general annual festivals, the Irish people also held local patterns in honour of the patron saint of the district or else of some better known saint whose name was associated with a holy well or other ancient landmark in the parish. These patterns were important social occasions in olden days, and the countryside is the poorer for their passing. Relatively few are still held with the same religious fervour and large attendance as of old; indeed, in most places the old centres of popular devotion are almost forgotten, save by a few elderly people who still cling to the former practices.

Holy wells were usually situated near the ruin of an old church or monastic site. They may have been, in some cases, centres of some kind of prechristian ceremonies, later taken over by the early Church; in others, it is probable that they were domestic wells used by the monks and other clergy, thus acquiring special qualities in the eyes of the local population. The devotion, as expressed in patterns, consisted in the " paying of rounds " at the well: each pilgrim either prayed at the well-side in a kneeling position or else walked around the well or an adjacent mound, reciting a prescribed number of Paters and Aves. The water was sipped at the end of the " rounds " and some of it was taken away in bottles. Offerings of coins, medals, pieces of cloth, flowers and other objects were left at the well-side by pilgrims. Some wells were supposed to have special powers for the healing of certain ailments.

In the old days, hundreds, if not thousands, of people attended patterns. After they had " paid their rounds ", they enjoyed themselves in the company of friends, drinking, dancing, and eating the food and fruits on sale at booths nearby. Fighting was more common then than it is now, and when factions of rival groups met at patterns, some became very disorderly, and both the law and the Church tried to abolish the abuses. In the process, not only the abuses, but also the patterns themselves tended to come into disfavour, leading to their almost total extinction in recent decades.

As well as patterns, pilgrimages were very popular religious functions in Ireland. The two great ones which still flourish are that to Lough Derg, in Co. Donegal, extending from June 1 to August 15, and the pilgrimage to the summit of Croagh Patrick in Mayo on the Sunday nearest to August 1. Many other pilgrimages to centres such as Glendalough (Co. Wicklow), Mám Éan (Co. Galway), Glencolmcille (Co. Donegal) and Mount Brandon (Co. Kerry), to name but a few, were of great local importance in former times, but like so many patterns, these too have lost their ancient patronage.

Dr. A. T. Lucas, Director of the National Museum of Ireland, and Francis Joseph Bigger have written interesting monographs about Irish Penal Crosses (of wood, with emblems of the Passion engraved), which are found in Ireland. Lucas thinks that they were carved as souvenirs for pilgrims to take home after making a pilgrimage to Lough Derg; each bears the date of the year with which it was concerned.

VIII. MAGIC AND OTHER POWERS

THE BELIEF IN Fate as a controlling power over human destiny seems to have been very strong in the popular mind from time immemorial. The time, place and other circumstances of one's birth were regarded as indicative of what was in store for the individual. Even certain places were believed to be subject to sinister influences, e.g. stray sods *(fóidíní mearbhaill)*; the belief that some houses or farms were dogged by ill-luck; or that certain lakes or parts of the seashore claimed a victim from time to time.

By acts of divination, too numerous to mention here, and by the observation of certain signs and omens, people tried to foretell the future and to forestall threatened evils by magic acts. Magic may be termed the use of certain words or actions by human beings which, it was hoped, would produce results beyond their normal effect. It was man's attempt to change or nullify the intentions and actions of evilly-disposed powers, and to bring about a beneficent result. The warding-off of evil and the protection of one's happiness and prosperity were the main objects of sorcery and magic. Thousands of different techniques were used in this connection in Ireland and else-where, involving the carrying out of otherwise normal acts, but now accompanied by an involved traditional ritual. The aims of these acts of sorcery were very numerous: to avert or cure sickness in man and beast; to avoid ill-luck and promote the chances of good luck; to bring about the defeat or death of an enemy; to raise or calm a storm; to acquire extraordinary power or knowledge; to send ill-luck to an enemy; to steal a neighbour's " profit "; to sink boats or ships; to render oneself invisible; to banish rats, mice or other vermin; to produce love or attraction; to restrain or overcome evil spirits or fairies; and scores of other objects which were deemed important for one's luck and prosperity. Sacrifice of birds and animals was, as we have seen, carried out at certain festivals, and offerings of other kinds also played a part. The more bizarre and complicated the actions intended to produce the desired results, the more certain they were, it was thought, to prove successful.

So uncertain was man's life in early times that it will cause no wonder to learn that he looked about him for help from any quarter to restore his confidence. Thus arose the belief that certain human beings were endowed with special powers for good, but also, unfortunately, for evil. Some were thought to possess these powers from birth: posthumous children; those born under a certain planet; seventh sons, and those born with the evil eye or powers of second sight. Others had power because of their surname: Cahills, Keoghs, Walshes, Cassidys, O'Heneys and so on. Priests were regarded as having powers far beyond what their ordination had conferred on them: powers to control bad landlords, " profit " stealers, evil spirits, fairies and the Devil himself; silenced priests were said to be exceptionally powerful. Persons with healing powers were abundant, and were much in vogue. So too were poets for their powers of satire and their ability to banish rats (this attribution of power was general in Ireland and in many other countries too). Then there were " wise " men and women who knew of things that were happening far away, and who were said to be able to foretell the future (it was thought that they acquired these gifts through their association with the fairies). There were men who could raise or calm storms, who could cause women to follow them, and who by their evil eye, tongue or wish could bring misfortune on others. Women, too, had exceptional powers in many fields for either good or evil.

Man also looked to certain objects to protect him against ill-luck and produce beneficial results. No list of these talismans could hope to be exhaustive. It will suffice to mention just a few: iron (plough, nails, horseshoe, tongs); certain types of money, rings, pins, knives (black-handled), needles, and edged weapons generally; cloths and garments of certain kinds (white cloth, red ribbon, *brat Bhríde*, garments associated with priests); threads and ropes; stones (associated with saints, cursing-stones, quern stones); clay (from graves, or blessed by a priest); herbs and plants ("hungry grass" which produced hunger in those who trod on it unsuspectingly, house-leek, four-leafed shamrock, *seamar Mhuire,* seed of fern and flax); trees (hazel, bean-berry, rowan); oatmeal and salt (as protection against fairies); fire; certain kinds of water (forge-water, feet-water, water found in a stone-hollow, boundary water); certain products of birds and animals (goose-grease, skin of a king-otter, fox-tongue, shoulder-blade of a sheep, foot of goat or rabbit, eggs); religious objects (emblems, medals, candles, "gospels", crosses, holy water); objects associated with the human body (hair, caul, blood, spittle, urine); objects associated with the dead (dead hand, skull, herb from graveyard, leavings after a wake); and hundreds of other amulets and talismans.

There was also much lore and many customs and beliefs associated with particular emblems and symbols. A few of these will suffice: the exhibition of a bush to signify that a ship or a cart of turf was for sale, or (in the case of Puck Fair in Ireland and others abroad) the hoisting of a goat or other symbol to denote the starting-point and conclusion of a fair; marks on animals or goods to show that they had been sold; dress worn by married women only; various marks on the forehead or other parts of the body on certain occasions; effigies and emblems taken from house to house at certain festivals; emblems of death, of defiance, of surrender, or of victory; emblems connected with work (last sheaf, harvest knots, emblems worn by labourers for hire); rings, squares, triangles, prints of feet, hands or fingers; crosses drawn or made at certain times; knots of various kinds; and the drawing of lots by various means. Numbers and colours, too, had their lore, but this cannot be described here.

There were also many customs and beliefs connected with speech and silence. The power of the tongue (for cursing, partial praise, blessing, swearing, the telling of truth or falsehood) attracted much lore. So too did the name a person had: some names were lucky or the opposite; some names were tabu to mention on certain occasions, as we have already mentioned; the name was used much in folk medicine; and it featured in many customs and beliefs associated with death and burial.

The recitation of charms (debased or apocryphal folk prayers) was very common in Ireland up to recent decades. They were generally known to, and applied by, only certain persons to whom they had been traditionally handed on, and were much in evidence in attempts to heal certain ailments. The Irish term for a charm was *ortha* (Latin *oratio*). They were used for many purposes apart from healing: for protection (*ortha an chiorraithe*, against the evil eye), for stealing the " profit " from neighbours or preventing same, for edging scythes and other implements, for banishing rats, changelings, etc., and for many other purposes. Their use has now died out almost completely. I remember how as boys, we set " cradle-birds " *(cliabháin éan)* to catch blackbirds and thrushes, and if we caught only a robin or some bird which we did not want, we let it go while we whispered to it: " robin, robin, I'll let you go, and bring me home a blackbird ". This was probably one of the last uses of a charm which I have met.

Finally, mention must be made of the traditional code of right and wrong which was strictly observed by country people. The breaking of a tabu was believed to be followed inevitably by retribution. Among the wrong acts listed were sacrilege of any kind (interference with holy persons, places and things), profanation of the Sabbath, desecration of holy wells, interference with the fairies (building on a fairy-path, or digging up a *lios*, " fairy fort ", or abusing a fairy bush or tree), harming animals or birds of a special kind (seals, seagulls, molesting dumb creatures), keeping late hours, speaking wrongly (telling secrets, unreasonable fault-finding, praising some work before it has been completed or half-heartedly praising something, using forbidden names or words), mocking and mimicry, murder, dishonesty, and many others.

IX. "THE WORLD OUTSIDE US"

AS ALREADY STATED, man has always lived in fear of the unknown, mainly because he felt that his fate and condition were subject to the whim of dangerous powers beyond his efficient control. True, he did try to influence them by offering sacrifice, as well as by his own valiant, but precarious, attempts at magic. In this final chapter, something will be said about the nature of these powers—let us call them supernatural beings—and the categories into which they may be divided.

First of all, comes the Devil. In folktales, he is generally a figure of fun, who is outwitted and foiled in his attempts to gain possession and control of human beings. This is not so in folk belief, however. There he is something to be feared. He may appear in human form (as a card-player, as sponsor at baptism, even in the guise of the Virgin or the Pope), or in the shape of an animal (a goat, or a dog). He was said to haunt certain places, to have built certain bridges, and to have left his mark here and there on the landscape (The Devil's Bit in Co. Tipperary, for example). His evil activities knew no bounds; he possessed people while they were still alive, or else tried to win their souls after they had died; and priests, as well as other human beings, with the aid of prayer and holy water, tried to cope with him.

Hags, such as *Cailleach Bhéara* (The Hag of Béara), and giants, belong rather to mythology than to recent folk belief. The idea of giants seems to have arisen through people seeing huge boulders and standing stones thrown in strange positions, which could only be explained by the action of some huge beings—people did not believe, however, that giants ever

81   F

existed. So too, there were legends about warriors who slept in caves or castles, waiting for the call to free their country, as in the Barbarossa story.

It is when we come to the fairies that we confront a belief which is perhaps as old as man himself, and which is still strong even in our own day in rural areas. If I am asked whether I believe in fairies, I reply by saying that the question should be framed in another way: Do I believe that our ancestors, and the older people of the present generation, sincerely held such a belief? My answer is definitely Yes. What one believes strongly in is something real and factual for him, however others may decry it. The real point about belief in the fairies is: Why should it ever have arisen? And the answer would seem to be that belief in the existence of the fairy world helped to solve, in a kind of sensible way, problems which were beyond explanation in a purely rational way. People always looked for causes for everything that happened, and if some otherwise unexplainable occurrence could be ascribed to fairy agency, they felt relieved and comforted.

The fairies were then a reality for our ancestors. They had various names in Irish, connoting The Good People, The Little People, The Noble People, The People of the Hills, The People Outside Us, and so on. They were said to live in the lisses (abandoned former homesteads, of which there are thousands throughout the country), as well as in raths, moats and hills. Their origin was ascribed to the fall of the angels from Heaven after Lucifer had rebelled against God; when St. Michael appealed to the Almighty not to empty Heaven altogether, He relented and allowed the angels (fallen or otherwise) to remain where they were: those who had by that time fallen to earth remained there—these are our fairies—

while those who were still falling live in the air. They are worried as to their fate on the last day, and a story explains that if they have enough blood in their bodies (and they have not) with which even to write their names, they will be allowed to enter Heaven on the Day of Judgement.

Some people were believed to have the power of seeing them, others not. In appearance, they were generally of human stature, except the lone figure among them, the leprechaun shoemaker (a much-exaggerated being), who was diminutive. The fairies led a community life, having their own local rulers: Finnbheara and Méadhbh in Connaught, Clíodhna in Munster, Áine in Donegal and so on. They seemed to live like human beings, using much the same kind of food, and having a taste for such things as tobacco and whiskey or poteen. When the latter was being secretly distilled, the first drops of it were always thrown against the roof as a libation for Red Willie, one of the fairies, who would then lead the gaugers and police astray; if, however, Willie were ignored in this regard, he would lead the police to where the still was located. Fairies were said to borrow food from their human neighbours, if short, and would also borrow the use of a cow and milk her in the liss. They always returned what they had borrowed, however, whether it be a vessel or the equivalent of some food. They were said to work in much the same way as their human neighbours, sowing their own crops, doing their own spinning and weaving and so on. And their help was forthcoming, it was said, if a kindly neighbour was in need.

They were thought to move their residence from one liss or fort to another at certain chief festivals. As they might be in the neighbourhood of a house at any time, people gave warning to them when they threw out ashes or dirty water, and discon-tinued any action to which the fairies objected. They travelled about from place to place too; in folktales, they went on the backs of horses which they had magically created from *buachallán* (ragwort) plants, whenever they wished to travel over to London, Paris or Spain and further afield on some mission. Indeed, the first cart is said to have been introduced into Ireland through their agency !

They had their own cattle too, as well as horses, and there are many stories about the fine breeds of both which resulted from the mating of farmers' and fairies' stocks. They bought and sold cattle at fairs too, in the guise of human beings, and took part unseen in the fun and bustle of the fair. Farmers did not resent unduly the milking of their cows occasionally by the fairy folk, but when the little people tried to take fine cows away into their world, leaving sickly ones behind, every effort was made to prevent this or to recover the abducted animals by threatening to dig up the fairy fort. One of the ways in which fairies were supposed to take cattle from farmers was by throwing arrows at them, causing them to be " elf-shot ".

Not only did the fairies ride, hunt and race against one another; they also played games of hurling against opponents, always winning if they had a human being as one of their team. They also sang, played music and danced in the fairy forts, and some human musicians were said to have acquired their exceptional skill from them. They were always ready with help and advice for those of their human neighbours whom they liked.

But they could also be mischievous and even vindictive. They set people astray, impeded at night people whom they did not like, frightened poachers, and played pranks of various kinds. They could be harmful too. The potato blight was ascribed to their agency, as were various kinds of illness ("fairy stroke", blasts and blemishes and so on) and the loss of " profit " in milk and butter. I have already referred to some of the many antidotes used to combat them, especially when they attempted to take away human beings (such as women in childbed and male children), cattle, and crops. People were not sorry to learn that in their own world, they were not free from strife and wars; white blood was said to have been often seen on the ground after a fairy battle at night.

The most dreaded group among the fairies was " the fairy host " *(an slua sí)*, which often went about in the form of a " fairy wind " and took a human being along with them when they set out on their journeys, often with evil intent. These human beings seemed to be necessary for the success of the enterprise, be it the stealing of crops, the abduction of a bride, the winning of a game, or the wreaking of vengeance on somebody who had displeased them. They were said by the neighbours to be " in the fairies ", and might be either men or women. From their association with the *slua sí*, they were regarded with both awe and respect by their neighbours, who, however, were glad to avail themselves of their advice and help when all else failed.

Besides the lisses or " fairy forts ", of which there are scores of thousands in Ireland, fairies were also said to live in many other places, known as *áiteanna uaisle* ("noble places"). Many mountains and hills in Ireland were particularly associated with the good people (Cnoc Meá, Sliabh na mBan, Cnoc Áine and Cnoc Fírinne are examples). Raths, moats, and *dúin* (larger than lisses) were also looked upon as fairy dwellings. There were stories too about " fairy rings " in fields, "fairy paths", "fairy palaces", "fairy trees" and bushes, as well as underground chambers and rooms within the bosom of rocks. Into any or all of these human beings might be abducted to replenish the fairy stock; some were said to have been rescued; others either died in fairyland (midnight funerals were often said to be related to this), or else were sent back to die on earth in the guise of old cows or other animals.

One of the commonest beliefs in connection with the abduction of human beings or animals by fairies was that, when they took off the healthy person or animal, they left instead some sickly substitute, known as an *iarlais* or changeling. This belief would seem to have grown from the rational cause for a decline in human or animal health being misunderstood— if a person or animal began to waste away, they were regarded as not human or animal any longer but as changelings. There was at least one case of such a person being burned to death, as the main means adopted for banishing such unwelcome beings were either fire or running water.

Another intriguing aspect of fairy belief was concerned with *leannáin sí*, fairy lovers. It might work either way: a human falling in love with a supernatural being, or vice versa. A good example is the legend of Inchiquin Castle in Co. Clare, where the fairy wife left when her husband had broken her tabu against the invitation of visitors to the castle—a story told in other countries also.

Spirits played an important part in the traditional beliefs of our forefathers. They were difficult to identify, so far as one can judge. Many of them seemed to be of an evil disposition, having been condemned, it was thought, for some heinous crime, e.g., putting an unbaptised child to death. Their punishment was regarded as everlasting, hence their malice towards humans who met them late at night. Many of them seemed to be bound to certain places (possibly where their supposed crimes were committed), and thus got to be known as Sprid na Bearnan (The Spirit of the Gap, in Co. Limerick), Petticoat Loose, in the Decies of Munster, *Sprid Charraig an Eidhin* (The Spirit of Carriganine, in South Kerry), and so on. One spirit, known as *Sprid an Tobac* (The Spirit of the Tobacco), always offered a smoke of tobacco to men whom she met, and could only be finally released from her suffering by the recipient reciting *paidir an tobac* (the tobacco prayer), offered after smoking for the souls of the dead. Spirits could be restrained or banished, it was thought, by such various means as holy water, a black-handled knife, an iron chain, a hazel stick, a cock, a true mare *(fíor-láir)*—seventh in direct line of succession—and many others. Priests were thought to be especially successful in ridding places of spirits, by banishing them to some narrow confine (between the froth and the water, between the bark and the wood of a tree, or to the Red Sea). Spirits could appear in male or female form, the latter being the more formidable, or else as various animals or birds.

While it is difficult to distinguish between the nature of spirits *(sprideanna)* and ghosts *(taisí, taidhbhsí)*, the latter appeared to be less malicious, save in their wish to take the living away with them. They were thought to be suffering some kind of temporary punishment for less serious crimes than those ascribed to spirits, or else to be anxious to return to their former places of residence for some particular purpose. These reasons were many: to fulfil a promise given before death, to seek help of some kind, to revisit friends (relatives, lover), to take revenge on somebody, to help relatives in trouble, and so on. They generally appeared in human form, so far as can be ascertained in such indefinite matters.

While the term *púca* (puck) is generally applied to a fairy or spirit, the name really seems to properly belong to a super-natural animal, which took men on nightmare rides at night, leaving them home exhausted at the dawn of day. It would appear that the *púca* itself was afraid of spirits, and in some cases was helpful to human beings. The nightmare *(an tromluí)* was regarded as something in the shape of a bird which spread its wings over the sleeper. Many charms were invoked against it, such as:

> *Anna, máthair Mhuire, Muire, máthair Chríost,*
> *Eilís dhea-oibreacha, máthair Eoin Baiste :*
> *Cuirim an triúr so idir mé agus galar na leapa,*
> *Idir mo mhúchadh, mo bhádhadh nó mo bhascadh.*
> *Cuirim an Chrois ar ar céasadh Críost*
> *Idir mé agus an tromluí go maidin.*

(Anne, mother of Mary, Mary, mother of Christ, Elizabeth the well-doer, mother of John the Baptist : these three I place between me and the malady of the bed, suffocation, drowning or injury. I place the Cross on which Christ was crucified between me and the nightmare until morning !)

Other supernatural manifestations included *an cholann gan ceann* (the headless body), which seemed destined to wander about in search of its head. There was also *an cóiste bodhar* (the silent coach), which appeared to be drawn by headless horses and came to fetch away unpopular persons, such as bad landlords, when they died. Then there were supernatural funerals, seen at night by late home-comers or other travellers. They were variously explained as being *(a)* funerals made up of dead persons who were bringing home for burial the body of somebody who had died far away, or *(b)* funerals of humans who had died in fairyland.

The under-water world was also inhabited in popular belief. Anchors might be caught under the thresholds of houses deep under the waters, and the sea-woman who lived there would try to detain, as husband, the sailor sent down to free them; or a child of the sea might be taken in a fisherman's net; or a fishing-hook would haul up from the sea-bed a sprig of heather on which a honey-bee was busy at work. Men rose out of the sea to warn fishermen of an approaching storm. The mermaid came out of the sea to comb her hair, laid aside her *cochall* (hood) which was then snatched by a local man, whom she had to follow home; she bore him children too, but, on recovering her hood, she took it off into the sea with her. Unions between humans and water-beings were said to produce offspring who were sleepless and web-footed. The sea, lakes and rivers all had their stocks of animals: cows, bulls, pigs, dogs and horses, as well as monster eels and *piastaí* (serpents). Many stories are told of the emergence of these creatures from their watery home to graze or to mate with land animals (in the case of cows, bulls and horses) or to ravage countrysides in the case of eels and serpents.

Supernatural places were said to exist both under water and on land. Off the coast of Galway, an island, named *Beag-Árainn* (Little Aran), would be laid bare by the sea once every seven years, and could be disenchanted only by the touch of natural fire; so too were mentioned *Cill Stuithín*, off the coast of Clare, and many other enchanted lands. There were also stories about sunken towns and cities (at *Tonn Tóime* in Dingle Bay, at Bannow, Co. Wexford, at Lough

Neagh, and several other places). Belief in the existence of fairy palaces, supernatural houses and castles, and haunted houses of various kinds was very strong in former times. So too was the belief in hidden treasure, usually guarded by some strange cat or eel or other creature; some of this hidden wealth was said to have been left behind by the "Danes" (Vikings).

Other beliefs concerned supernatural manifestations of various kinds: eerie sounds (rappings, cries, music and such); strange lights seen where they should not be in normal circumstances (for example, phosphorescent gases in bogs gave rise to the being called Will of the Wisp); supernatural objects of many kinds met at night; phantom ships and boats; sky and weather phenomena; and hundreds of other strange things which gave rise to stories of eerie adventures.

Ideas about the end of the world abounded also. It would take place when a certain castle fell, when the sea had covered a still dry area, when the places of the fallen angels were filled in Heaven, and so on. Of course, the occurrence of plagues, wars, strange prodigies or natural phenomena were regarded as omens of the final dissolution too. Old prophecies, such as those ascribed to Colmcille and Malachi, had great vogue. Purgatory, for those whose souls were not yet fit for Heaven, was often spent on earth, and many stories were told about it by our forefathers. In olden times, Hell seems to have been regarded as a place of cold, rather than fire (*Ifreann fuar, fliuch*— Hell, cold and wet); and so far as folktales were concerned, souls could be freed from it on certain occasions. A meteor falling through the night sky was said to denote the entry of a soul to Heaven; rain on a funeral day was regarded as a good omen for the soul of the deceased; and, finally, there were even graveyards where all the dead buried there were assured of Heaven.

Finally, mindful of the comforting tradition that God will allow St. Patrick to judge the Irish on the Last Day, we leave the field of Irish folk custom and belief for the present.

BIBLIOGRAPHY

The Festival of Lughnasa, Máire Mac Neill.
A Handbook of Irish Folklore, Seán Ó Súilleabháin.
Irish Popular Superstitions, Sir William Wilde.
Irish Folk Ways, E. Estyn Evans.
The Voyage of Bran, ed. Kuno Meyer.
Penal Crosses, A. T. Lucas.
Irish Penal Crosses, Francis J. Bigger.

SAOL AGUS CULTÚR IN ÉIRINN

The following booklets have been published in this series: